This isn't just love—it's legacy.

WHEN *God* *Wrote* US

A LOVE STORY HEALED BY FIRE.
REBUILT BY FAITH

When God Wrote Us

A Novel by Muriel Godfrey

Dedication & Acknowledgments

First and foremost, I give all honor and glory to God—my source, my sustainer, my everything. Without Him, there would be no story to tell, no strength to write, and no light to shine. He is the Author of it all.

To my incredible family and friends—thank you for being my safe space, my inspiration, and my unwavering support system. Truth is, my friends are my family—chosen and cherished. Your love has carried me through every chapter of my life.

This first novel is tenderly and triumphantly dedicated... to me.
Muriel, I'm so proud of the woman you have become. You have quite literally fought through hell, held on to heaven, and risen with fire in your bones. May you continue to prosper in God and forever soar and elevate.

To my beautiful mother—Mommy, I miss you so much. I thank you for everything. May you continue to rest. Your love blessed me in ways words can't capture, and I love you so much.
To my incredible father—thank you for being such an amazing man. First to yourself, then to Mama, and then to me and my sister. I know you've been a rock for so many others too, but "thank you" doesn't seem like enough. I love you immensely, Dad. Also—thank you for raising a genius (insider). Your wisdom lives in me.
To my sisters and all my other God-sent sisters—your sisterhood is a gift I never take for granted.
To my little big sister—thank you for being so amazingly you. Only you could be born after me and still be the boss.
To my big sister—thank you for paving the way and helping me get it

right. Your strength has always been a guidepost.

To my God-sister—my loving box of chocolate. You are sweet, strong, and full of surprises. I treasure you deeply.

To my amazing best friend since 6th grade—you've seen me through every awkward stage, wild season, and winning moment. I love you, girl. Thank you for being a forever one.

To my amazing nieces and nephews—y'all keep me laughing, praying, and feeling young(ish). Auntie loves you more than you know!

To my incredible Mother-in-Love—thank you for your spirit, your prayers, your presence, and your everything.

To all of my in-loves—thank you for being your authentic selves, for embracing me, and for adding so much joy to this journey.

To our six amazing children—you are not just my legacy; you are a living, breathing extension of my heart. You are the rhythm in my walk, the light in my fire, and the reason I push to become better every single day. I thank God for choosing me to mother such greatness.

To our grandchildren, great-grands, and those still to come: I love you beyond words.

To my aunts, uncles, and cousins—shoutout to this phenomenal bloodline we come from!

To my Pastor, my First Lady, and every one of my amazing church families—thank you for your covering, your teaching, your love, and your constant encouragement. Y'all don't just pray—you cover with power!

To every friend, every mentor, every divine connection, every stranger-turned-assignment, and yes... even to those who tried it—thank you! You helped shape this story too. Whether you poured into me or pushed me closer to God, I count it all joy. I love everyone God has allowed me to cross paths with—friends, family, and even foes. (And yes, even the ones I had to block... temporarily. Growth is real!)

To my Forever Soaring and Elevating family—this movement was born out of pain, purpose, and a promise. Thank you for believing in the call, carrying the vision, and helping others rise with me. This isn't just a name—it's a mantle. And we carry it with fire.

To the reader holding this book in your hands—thank you. Whether you stumbled upon this story or were divinely led here, I pray it blesses you, heals something in you, and reminds you that your story isn't over. You are seen, you are loved, and you are not alone.

And last, but never least... to the man who plays my heartbeat every time he drums—my husband.
Words fail me when it comes to you. I could write an entire book trying to express all that you are to me... and maybe I will one day.
Maybe I have.
But for now, I'll simply say:
Thank you, babe. You already know.
I love you.

And to everyone—family, friend, reader, or even foe—I love you. Truly. You were a part of the making of this message, and for that, I'm grateful.

Table of Contents

THE DEEPER YOU GO, THE MORE YOU KNOW
The Deep Calleth Unto the Deep

Introduction

I always said I would have a daughter named Miera.
Life gave me three beautiful daughters—each radiant in their own
right—yet none of them carry that name.

But Miera?
She lives.
She breathes through these pages.
And her name, of Hebrew origin, means "giving light" or "shining."
That's exactly what she does.

Though this series is fictional, the heartbeat of these stories is very real.
Many moments are born from my own journey—bruised but not broken,
tested but still standing. What was meant to crush me became the oil
that flows through every chapter. What was meant to silence me became
a sound—a war cry for every woman who's ever dared to love, to fall, to
rise, and to become.

Miera's story is a reflection of the battles we fight behind closed doors,
the questions we're too scared to ask out loud, and the hope we hold onto
even when everything else slips through our fingers.

This isn't just a novel.
It's a light.
A divine invitation.
An echo from Heaven saying, "You are not alone. You are not forgotten.
And yes—He still writes beautiful endings."

So as you read, I pray you do more than relate. I pray you remember.
Remember who you are.
Remember whose you are.
And remember the promise that still stands:
"For I know the plans I have for you," declares the Lord... —Jeremiah 29:11

Welcome to When God Wrote Us.
This is not just her story.
It's yours, too.

Chapter 1: It All Started Simple...

"Do not despise these small beginnings, for the Lord rejoices to see the work begin."
— Zechariah 4:10

Every Girl Has a Plan......

Growing up, the old folks used to say,
"If you want to make God laugh, tell Him your plans."

I never understood what that meant. Thought it was just one of those tired sayings, soaked in wisdom and worn-out stories. Something the elders said while sipping coffee on front porches, watching life pass by.

But life has a funny way of humbling you.
Turns out, the joke was on me.

I never imagined the twists, turns, and trauma I'd survive.
Over the years, people would say things like,
"Miera, you're so strong."
"You're resilient. You really should write a book."

They meant it as a compliment. But to me, writing a book meant something far more terrifying—it meant reliving it. It meant digging up pain I buried beneath strength and smiles.

And yet, here I am.
Writing. Reflecting. Wrestling with a hard truth:
Am I really healed... or just really good at pretending?

Most of my life didn't go as planned.
So now I'm choosing to write it out—one truth at a time.

There was always something different about me. Not in a bragging way—more like a knowing.

A quiet, deep sense that I was *set apart*.
Took me a while to realize that it wasn't just *me*—it was the God within me.

I was born and raised in Chicago. The real Chicago.
Before it got renamed "Chiraq."
Back when folks would lie and say they were from the Chi just to add a little weight to their story.

I always hated that nickname—Chiraq.
It highlights the pain but ignores the beauty.
Because Chicago? It raised me. Loved me. Taught me.

I came from a two-parent household with **flawed but phenomenal** parents.
Family dinners looked like reunions—every weekend. Loud, loving, and laced with laughter.

Some people doubted I'd make it far.
But here I am. Still standing. Still shining.
And if my story can help you keep going—then it's worth every word.

By 16, I had it all mapped out:

- ■ Doctor of Pharmacy
- ■ Marry a fine man who loved me like my daddy loved my mama
- ■ Build an empire
- ■ Live happily ever after

I was already working part-time, bringing home checks that made grown folks jealous. $900 here, $1,000 there—if I really went hard.

I worked at **The Lark**, one of the most exclusive clothing stores in Ford City Mall—**Chicago's hidden gem**. That mall had a whole vibe. Families came dressed up just to window-shop. The food smelled like joy. The energy? Electric.

I'd arrive early just to walk through, soaking in the scent of churros and cinnamon almonds. It felt like I belonged to something big. Something beautiful.

My boss, Licia Thompson?
She was a boss chick in every sense. The kind of woman who handled business and didn't waste words. Her assistant Cassie was solid too.

And me? I wasn't your average sales associate. I didn't sell dreams or lie to customers for commission.
If an outfit wasn't flattering, I said so—**with love**.
"Nice fit, but not for you," I'd say with a grin.
Respectfully.

It got to a point where the ballers came looking for me.
Tell me what event you're going to—I'll dress you like royalty. And they always left with the whole look.
The tips? Heavy.

But I wasn't just feeding the streets.
I was feeding my home, too.

I love hard. I give harder.
I used my earnings to bless my parents with paid utility bills and fresh fits. I left receipts on the dresser with love notes.
They'd fuss, but they were proud.

My little sister? She just needed a few outfits and a little pocket change. I was happy to be her "sister-slash-sponsor."

On weekends, me and my girls were **outside**.
We were small in number, but mighty.
If I was the driver, you were guaranteed speed and thrill.
They called me the rollercoaster ride.
I'd laugh and say,
"But did you die, though?"

My circle? Solid.
Five women. One man. All real.

- **Kiesha** – my god-sister, my ride or die.

- **Lola** – my blunt, bold, beautiful cousin-friend.

- **Lila** – my baby sister, my heart on two legs.

- **Nola** – my sixth-grade bestie, my forever friend.

- **Nija** – smart, stylish, and straight up.

- **Fitzgerald** – my day-one homie... loyal to the core.

Everyone in my life earned their place.
I don't do fake. I don't force.
And one thing life taught me:
Not everybody deserves access to your heart.

Before high school? Oh, I was getting roasted daily like a Sunday pot roast.
Kids had jokes for **everything**—my skin, my hair, my outfits, even how I walked.

I got called:

- "Nappy-headed."

- "Slave."

- "Poor."

Like... not "on a budget," not "low-income," just **POOR.**
They used to say it with their whole chest too, like they were delivering breaking news.

And the wild part? My parents could afford all the name brands. I just wasn't pressed.
If I liked it, I wore it. Period.
I was out here pairing **Kmart leggings with Dollar Tree confidence**—and I thought I was killin' it.
Turns out... they didn't see the vision.

I had this one outfit with glittery butterflies and capris that stopped at that awkward mid-shin spot. I loved it. It felt like destiny. The girls at school? Not so much.
One girl said I dressed like I was raised on *PBS Kids and struggle.*
Another said my hair looked like a "bush that got hit with holy water but didn't get delivered."
And yet, **they still copied my homework.**
Make it make sense.

But through it all—I stayed at the top of my class.
Straight A's, big dreams, and a mouth that would check you in cursive if you played with me.
They hated what they couldn't control.

What didn't kill me?
Built a version of me they'd never be ready for.

And then came Nola.

She transferred to my school in sixth grade.
Light-skinned, long curly hair, pretty smile—**the type who could've easily joined the Mean Girl Olympics.**
So, naturally, I didn't trust her.
In my head, I was already preparing for the day she'd switch sides and join the bullies.
But she never did.

She sat next to me on the first day like she already knew I was her people.
She wasn't impressed by the cliques, the chaos, or the cafeteria politics.
She chose **me**—not for clout, not for convenience, but because she saw me.

And that?
That changed everything.

I remember thinking, *"Okay God... I see You."*

Nola came in solid. No drama. No fake love.
She laughed at my corny jokes, complimented my outfits (even the butterfly one), and let me be fully me.

That was the beginning of something real.
No contracts. No explanations. Just **loyalty at first vibe.**

But I had learned to clap back or fall silent—depending on the day.
My mouth was slick. My boundaries? Firm.

So yeah, that's how it all started.
In a mall. With a circle. In a city that made me strong.
In a body that carried both trauma and truth.
With plans I made. And a God who would later rewrite them.

Chapter 2: It Gets Deep

"Before I formed you in the womb I knew you, before you were born I set you apart."
— Jeremiah 1:5

"Some people walk into your life like a whisper. Others show up like a plot twist."
— Unknown

When it came to Fitzgerald...
He wasn't just fine. He was **frustratingly fine.**
But more than that—he was *different.*

Most guys saw a girl like me—cute, confident, and curvy—and immediately turned into walking red flags.
Lust in their eyes. Game on their lips.
They wanted a body, not a bond.
A moment, not a mission.

But Fitzgerald?
He moved like a man with purpose.
There was a **stillness** about him—like peace wrapped in a fitted tee and prayer oil.
He didn't chase me. He **studied** me.
He saw me before I even knew I was being seen.

It wasn't just how he looked—it was how he *looked at me.*
Like I wasn't just beautiful. I was **divine.**
Like he didn't want to conquer me—he wanted to **cover** me.

He had this calm confidence, this subtle charm, this deep, unshakable wisdom
that made you want to sit still and listen.

And let's be clear—he was fine, but it was his **faith** that really turned heads.
A man that could pray *and* protect? Whew.

He didn't just ask for my number—he asked about my purpose.
Did I feel called to ministry?
What were my dreams?
What was my relationship with God like?

Sir... who sent you?

Fitzgerald came into my life like a soft storm—quiet but powerful.
And from that very first moment, I knew...
This wasn't gonna be a chapter.
This man might be the whole book.

But let me backtrack for a second...

I had just turned 16, and Granny came through heavy—bought me my first car.
Big win, right?

Well... I crashed it. Don't judge me.

It was me and Nola, headed to her mom's birthday party with a hot pan of spaghetti riding in the back seat. Some fool ran a stop sign and BOOM—spaghetti on the sidewalk, sauce everywhere, and the bumper? Gone.
RIP to my ride and Nola's mama's dinner.
Another story for another day.

Nola always said, "Whenever we're together, it's guaranteed to be an adventure."
And babyyy, she wasn't lying.

We met Fitzgerald on one of those **random, perfect summer days** when you just *know* something's about to happen.

Me and Nola decided to take the bus and hit up our favorite spot—**Ford City Mall**.
The sun was shining. Vibes were vibing. Hair was laid. Edges were respectful.
We shopped, laughed, flirted a little, and hit all our usual stores.

But something strange kept happening...

We kept running into the same group of guys.
They weren't exactly following us, but we kept crossing paths like some kind of rom-com rerun.

And every single time, I'd lock eyes with *one* of them.
Tall. Long locs. Chocolate skin. Eyes that said "I see you" without moving his lips.
And every time, I'd look away with a little laugh like, *Boy, don't gas yourself.*

That was Fitzgerald.

Fast forward to the end of the day.
Mall's closed. Feet tired. We hop on the bus to head home.

We're sitting in the back, decompressing from our mall marathon, when guess who walks on?

Yep. Him. And the whole gang.

They're loud. Confident. Doing too much.
I tried to act unbothered... until I felt it.
That stare.

I looked up—and boom. Eye contact.
He smiled. I looked away.

"I saw that," Nola said, grinning like a proud auntie.

"Saw what?" I rolled my eyes, trying to play it cool even as my face got warm.

Before I could change the subject, the bus pulled off.
That's when things took a turn.

"Nola... this doesn't look right."

She leaned forward, eyes wide. "Wait... where are we going?"
I looked out the window—**no landmarks, no street signs, just darkness and confusion.**

"Stay calm," I said. *My daddy always told me: Never panic first. Think first. React later.*

And then the boys started making their way to the back of the bus.
Nola was breathing like she was in labor. I stayed cool, but I was on alert.

Then Fitzgerald slid into the seat between us.

"You don't have to be scared," he said, his arm casually resting behind me. "We're here now. We got you."

I gave him a look and gently placed his hand back in his lap.
"Thanks. But I'm not scared. And my friend is just... dramatic."

He chuckled, unfazed. "I'm Fitzgerald. And you are?"

"Miera. And clearly, you've never heard of personal space."

That made him smile wider. Then he leaned in—and I caught it.
That scent.

Clean. Grown. Slightly sinful. **Whatever he was wearing needed a warning label.**

"I like you," he whispered.

"You don't even know me."

"Can I give you my number... so I can?"

Before I could respond, **Nola—being Nola—blurted out my whole number like she was reading off a coupon code.**
"773-624-1989."

"NOLA!" I snapped.

Fitzgerald laughed, already saving the number.
"She's gone be the one who keeps my lady in check," he said to her like they were already planning our wedding.

"I see both y'all done lost y'all minds," I muttered.

"She can be a little stubborn," Nola teased. "But I got you, Fitz. Know this though one wrong move and it's up. I don't play about mine."

"I hear you," Fitzgerald said, hands raised in surrender. "But something about this butterfly right here... I'm not letting that go."

"Y'all doing the most," I said. But secretly? I was enjoying every bit of it.

But I wasn't about to fall fast.
I met fly guys all the time. I wasn't new to charm—I was **raised around game**. So I hit him with a quick redirect.

"Didn't y'all come back here to *protect us*? Maybe help us figure out where we're going instead of flirting?"

He laughed and looked out the window. "Man, where *are* we? I got distracted watching you. I feel like we're on that show *Manifest*."

One of his boys shouted to the driver, "YO! Where we at?!"

No response.

I sighed. "Let me handle this."

Marched to the front like I owned the TA.

"Excuse me, Mr. Bus Driver... Why are we behind the mall?"

He looked at me through the mirror. "Made a wrong turn, sweetheart. We'll be back on route soon."

"Thank you." I turned and walked back like a calm queen.

When I sat down, Fitzgerald was grinning like I'd just proposed.

"I like how you handled that, beautiful."

"You don't quit, do you?"

"And you're learning," he said with a wink. "I come to win every time. I'm not going to stop pursuing you—even after I make you mine."

I raised an eyebrow. "You got confidence, I'll give you that."

As we rolled into 79th and Halsted, he stood up and called out:
"Miera! You better answer when I call to say goodnight!"

"Boy, bye," I said, biting a smile.

He leaned in one last time and whispered:
"The faster you run, the harder I chase. Goodnight, wifey."

The door closed and he kept his eyes on me the whole time the bus pulled off.

Nola screamed, "Yesssss, MiMi! You better ANSWER that call!"

"Nola," I rolled my eyes, "he doesn't even know me."

"Girl, he knows he likes you—and that's enough to start!"

"And you need to stop giving my number out like you, my PR manager."

"You should be thanking me for seeing what you're trying to act blind to."

I shook my head and stood up. "Let's go. This is our stop."

But inside?

Yeah, I was intrigued.

I wasn't about to say it out loud, but something about Fitzgerald pulled at me.

He had potential. I had my guard up.

And somewhere between the laughter and the chase...

I think God just dropped a plot twist.

Chapter 3: The Love that showed up

"Commit to the Lord whatever you do, and He will establish your plans."
— **Proverbs 16:3**

I had officially finished senior year—and I should've been floating.
You'd think with college on the horizon and my dreams finally unfolding, I'd be jumping for joy in slow motion, Beyoncé wind blowing through my hair.

But instead?
I felt like a roach under a flashlight.
Frozen. Anxious. Emotionally constipated.

It was the summer in the Chi—**that magical time** when the ice cream trucks sing louder, the aunties pull out the plastic patio furniture, and the fire hydrants become community swimming pools.

But instead of basking in it, I was stuck in my head.
On paper, everything looked perfect.
But my spirit? Heavy.

It felt like life was saying, "Congrats, girl! You made it! Now go start over somewhere far away from everyone and everything you love."

No thank you.

I was faking the excitement, giving "I'm good" responses, and praying nobody looked too closely. Of course, **Licia**—my boss, mentor, and unofficial life coach—saw through me immediately.

"You good, Miera?" she asked that afternoon, arms folded, brow raised like she was about to read me.

"Yeah, I'm good, boss lady," I said with my best fake smile. "Just thinking. College, new beginnings, it's a lot."

She didn't blink.
"Miera... you've been dreaming about this for years. Now it's here. You are more than ready. And let's not forget—you've got a wonderful man walking beside you."

I nodded. She was right.
But why did I still feel like I was holding my breath?

Fast forward to 8:59 PM. My shift was ending, and I remembered: Fitzgerald had dropped me off that morning. Which meant my car was at home... and *my man* was picking me up.

I walked outside—and there it was.

That all-black Benz, sitting pretty like it had an attitude. Red LED lights glowing beneath it like it just left a Fast & Furious audition.

I opened the door, and Fitzgerald leaned over with that signature smile.
"Good evening, beautiful. How was your day?"

"Fine," I mumbled, trying not to unpack my entire emotional suitcase.

He didn't buy it for one second.

"Mi, you know I can tell when you're lying, right?" he said, gently taking my hand and bringing it to his lips. "Talk to me, baby."

That's all it took.

Tears. Full breakdown. No warning.

I covered my face, annoyed with myself, but Fitz didn't flinch. He wiped my tears, tilted my chin, and said:

"Look at me. How many times have I ever broken a promise to you?"

I sniffed. "...Never."

"Exactly. I'm not starting now. You're not alone. We're in this together."

I thought we were headed home.
 But then... *we hit the expressway.*

"Where are we going?" I asked, side-eye sharp.

"I need to make a quick run," he said casually.

"See, this is how people end up on Dateline," I muttered.

He laughed and turned up the music.

Then came the questions—random and suspiciously deep:
 "Do you care about me?"

"Where do you see us in five years?"

"Do you know how much I love you?"

I gave sarcastic answers to keep things light, but this man wasn't playing.

The car ride was quiet for a moment, but not awkward. It was one of those rare silences where your soul gets to breathe. I could feel Fitzgerald glancing over at me, his fingers lightly drumming the steering wheel to the rhythm of the music.

We parked.

He looked at me and smirked. "Okay. I need you to trust me."

I narrowed my eyes. "Fitz... you better not be on no weird stuff."

He reached in the glove compartment—and pulled out a **blindfold**.

"Sir, I am a Black woman from the South Side of Chicago. You want me to do what?"

He laughed and leaned in closer. "Miera, I would never play you. I've planned something special. But I need your trust."

"See, this is how people get kidnapped," I said, squinting at him. "You really want me blindfolded? In heels?"

"I already brought the heels," he said, hopping out the car.

Heels?

He opened my door, knelt down, and started untying my gym shoes.

"Fitzgerald. If you mess up my edges or twist my ankle, I swear to google..."

He slipped off my shoes and replaced them with a pair of **nude stilettos**—then fastened a gold anklet with my name engraved in cursive. My heart tripped.

"I hate how good you are at this," I whispered.

"I love how easy it is to love you," he replied.

He blindfolded me gently, then kissed the center of my forehead like he was sealing a covenant. My nerves danced, but his presence covered me in peace.

"Okay, Ms. Lady. Let's go."

He led me carefully, whispering, "Step here... just a few more steps... stop."

The air changed. The scent of roses and vanilla hit me. The echo of my heels told me we were inside, somewhere big and open. Music hummed low in the background.

"I'm gonna lift you up—just for a moment," he said.

Before I could object, he picked me up like I was weightless and placed me in a plush chair.

Then I heard brushes. Blenders. **A makeup artist.**

"Whoever you are," I said out loud, "please don't have me out here looking like I'm ready for resurrection. I like soft, not spooky."

A soft laugh. Then Fitzgerald's voice. "Relax, baby. She got you."

I tried to act annoyed—but I was intrigued.

The MUA finished and said, "She's ready, Mr. Fitzgerald."

Next thing I knew, Fitz was back adjusting my earrings, fixing my necklace, and placing something soft and floral around my waist.

"Alright, alright," I said. "I've been real patient. I need answers."

He kissed my hand. "Patience is a virtue, baby."

We walked a few more steps. The music swelled. I heard it—**"This Is Why I Love You"** by MAJOR. My heartbeat kicked up.

"Okay, baby," he whispered. "I'm gonna take off your blindfold now."

He removed it slowly.

I blinked, letting the light settle, and then—

Wow.

The room glowed in gold and candlelight. Fairy lights sparkled across the ceiling like stars. A floor-to-ceiling sign read:
"Miera, You Got This—And We Got You."

I gasped. Everyone I loved was there—my parents, his family, my crew. Nola waved with tears in her eyes. My mama had her camera out. The whole room felt like a warm hug.

A surprise trunk party.

"You like it?" Fitzgerald whispered.

"I... I'm speechless."

"Well, don't cry yet," Nola shouted. "You'll mess up that face!"

I laughed through tears, overwhelmed. Fitz took my hand and walked me to a royal chair trimmed in gold.

He grabbed a mic. "Y'all, thank you for coming. This isn't just about gifts—it's about gratitude. Gratitude for the woman Miera is. For what she's overcome. For who she's becoming."

Cue more tears.

People began lining up—family, friends, church mothers, cousins. They spoke life over me, handed me dorm gifts, school supplies, encouragement. One even gave me an envelope with "Emergency Only" written on it. I peeked—it was a check.

Then Fitzgerald took the mic again.

He cleared his throat, but his voice was steady.

"Miera, I've loved you since that night on the bus. You thought I was playing, but I wasn't. That night, God spoke to me. I saw you. Not just your beauty, but your spirit. I've never met anyone like you."

He stepped down and handed me a **rose gold envelope**.

"This is the deed to your place near campus. I wanted to make sure you had a peaceful, private space to study, pray, and shine."

The room gasped. Cameras flashed. Nola screamed.

Then he handed me a **velvet box**. Inside: a **Mercedes-Benz EQS Maybach key.**

"Because queens don't Uber."

My jaw dropped. "You are... crazy. In the best way."

He dropped to one knee, pulled out another small box—and opened it to reveal a **massive pink diamond ring**, surrounded by delicate white diamonds shaped like angel wings.

The room fell silent.

"Miera Nielsen," he said, eyes glistening, "You are the woman I prayed for before I even knew how to pray. You are my peace, my partner, my answered prayer. Will you be my wife?"

I sobbed, nodded, then finally found my voice.

"YES!"

Cheers exploded. Music swelled. "Fortunate" by Maxwell played. My mama cried louder than me. Nola looked like she'd just caught the Holy Ghost. Fitz slipped the ring on my finger and pulled me into the softest, strongest hug.

"You did all this?" I whispered.

He held me close. "Every bit of it. For you. Because I love you. And because this is just the beginning."

Chapter 4: The Last Morning at Home

"See, I am doing a new thing! Now it springs up; do you not perceive it?"
— **Isaiah 43:19**

"Wake up, sissy—it's time to go!" Kiesha's voice dragged me out of my sleep like I owed her money.

"This is not the time for oversleeping," Lola chimed in, already snatching my covers back.

"Yeah, 'cause college life is different," Lila added. "We're not gonna be there to drag you out of bed every morning like this."

I cracked one eye open. "Why are all y'all in my room? And y'all better watch how you talk to me."

"Girl, we can't hear you through all that dragon breath," Lola said, waving her hand dramatically.

We all *lost it.* That was our classic inside joke—*"I can't hear you when you speak because your breath offends me."*

Still half-asleep and giggling, I got up, grabbed my shower bag, and mumbled, "Prosperous morning, Mom and Dad!" as the smell of turkey bacon and cinnamon grits filled the air.

"Prosperous morning, Miera!" my mom called back.

"Prosperous morning, sweetheart! Let's go—we gotta hit the road!" my dad added.

"Okay, Daddy!"

I showered, prayed my usual morning prayer—thanking God for breath in our bodies, peace in our house, and guidance on the journey—and got dressed.

When I checked my phone, a text from Fitzgerald was waiting:

> Good Morning, Beautiful.
> I know you're probably just getting dressed since you didn't answer my call.
> Remember—you got this.
> I'm already at the house making sure everything is set up. I packed your bags in your trunk already and got you a driver so you can ride with your family.
> I love you. Can't wait to see you.
> —Fitz

I smiled and replied:

> Prosperous Morning, Mr. Wonderful.
> You know me too well. Just made my bed, headed to the kitchen, then to the car.
> I love you.

I walked into the kitchen expecting the usual family breakfast setup, but my parents were packing everything into *to-go containers*.

"Wait, wait, wait. Why are we not eating now?" I asked, confused.

"Miera, we're already behind schedule," my mom said.

"We're not eating in my new car!" I gasped, offended.

"I told you she'd say that," my dad whispered to my mom.

"She'll be fine," she whispered back with a smirk.

"Mommy, please," I said softly. "Can we just sit and eat together? Like a family? Just one last time at home?"

Lola rolled her eyes. "Miera always gotta be extra."

I wasn't trying to be dramatic. I just loved the small moments. Maybe I was a little *extra*, but I believed in giving moments their full flowers—*extra love, extra laughs, extra gratitude.*

So my mom pulled the containers back out, laid down gold-trimmed plates and matching utensils—because even on the fly, presentation was everything in our house. We didn't just eat breakfast; we feasted like royalty.

We sat down and I asked, "So... what y'all gonna do while I'm away?"

"Same thing we always do," Lola answered. "Work, sleep, repeat. You act like you're being deployed."

"You gon' miss me first, Lola," I said with a grin.

"Whatever."

My dad chimed in, "We've already worked out a schedule with Fitzgerald for family nights every other weekend. We'll be seeing you more than you think."

After breakfast, we grabbed our things and headed outside—only to find a blacked-out luxury Sprinter van waiting in the driveway.

"Uh, Daddy... where's my car?"

"Fitzgerald took it to your new place early this morning. He sent the van so we could all ride together."

Nola burst out laughing. "And to think—you almost let that man pass you by! Miera, you better be grateful for me!"

"Shut up, Nola," I said, laughing. "I've always been grateful for you—even before Fitz showed up. Don't do too much."

I paused, looking around at my tribe—my parents, my sisters, my people.

"But most of all," I added, "I'm grateful to God. 'Cause only He could've pieced together something this beautiful... using all of us and our flaws."

"That's real," my dad said, nodding proudly.

We climbed into the van. The driver—a clean-cut man in a suit—greeted us all by name like we were VIPs. The van smelled like fresh roses. The leather was black with peanut butter stitching, soft lights glowing above, and in the middle of the cabin, a crystal vase with a single rose and a card tucked beneath it.

The card read:

You Got This.
—Fitz

I clutched it to my chest, fighting the tears. *Not right now, Miera. Hold it together.*

We got settled and the van pulled off. I stared out the window, then asked, "Y'all really gonna miss me?"

"We gon' see you every week," Nola said, matter-of-factly.

"I know," I replied. "But really—how do you feel? About me going off to college... becoming a wife... having a man that treats me like royalty? What do y'all really think?"

The van got quiet.

"I mean, it's not that far off from how we were raised," I said. "Daddy treated Mommy like a queen. Y'all just had simpler taste. Fitz? He believes in five-star everything. Sometimes it's a little flashy—but it's all love. It's never to show off—it's to show *me* how loved I am."

"Here she go again with the poetic stuff," Lola said, rolling her eyes.

"If that was deep, I'd drown," Lila joked.

"And y'all better learn how to swim, 'cause I'm not coming up for air," I said, smirking. "Now which one of y'all helping me unpack?"

Crickets.

Only my parents responded. "Well, we didn't come along just to wave goodbye," my dad said with a smile.

Laughter filled the van. The music turned up, the vibes were right, and for a moment, time slowed down.

This was it—my *last ride* before life would never be the same.

And I was ready.

Chapter 4, Part 2: *Can I Embrace the New?*

"Forget the former things; do not dwell on the past. See, I am doing a new thing! Now it springs up; do you not perceive it? I am making a way in the wilderness and streams in the wasteland."

-Isaiah 43:18-19

We pulled up to a **gated entrance**, and I swear I stopped breathing for a second.

Mouth open. Edges lifting. Spirit floating.

This wasn't a house. This was a *statement*.

Everyone in the van turned their heads, gasping like we'd just been transported into an episode of *Dream Homes of the Elite and Anointed*.

"Miera... oh my goodness," Lola whispered, pressing her face to the window.

Fitzgerald had been tight-lipped about the house—said he wanted me to experience it fresh. And *baby*, he did not disappoint.

The driver buzzed in, and the gate opened like the Red Sea parting. A winding brick road revealed itself, lined with glowing lights, sculpted hedges, and flowers that looked handpicked by angels.

We finally pulled into a **grand circular driveway** with stone lions on each side and towering double doors that screamed royalty. And on those doors was a sign:

"Welcome Home, Wifey."

I froze. The sign hit different. This wasn't just cute. It was sacred.

My whole body lit up with emotion—joy, shock, peace. But I kept my tears on standby. Not just yet.

"Dang, Miera... say something," Nola blurted after a long pause.

"For the first time in forever..." I whispered, "...I don't even know what to say."

My dad gently placed his hand on my shoulder, grounding me in the moment. I looked over at my mom—her lashes were catching tears, and her hand clung tightly to my dad's arm.

It was *too much* in the most beautiful way.

"Miera, what'd you say Fitzgerald does for a living again?" Lila asked, eyes still wide like a cartoon character.

"His family owns multiple construction companies," I replied simply.

Lola clutched her pearls like a church mother. "Ohhh! *Bro-in-law living the good life!*"

We all laughed.

The driver stepped out and opened the van door like we were the Obamas on inauguration day. As we climbed out, a man in a tailored suit with crisp white gloves greeted us at the steps.

"Good afternoon, Madam," he said, nodding to me. "**Welcome. I'm Brother Kevin. I've been instructed to escort you and your family on a private tour.**"

Of course Fitzgerald had a *Brother Kevin*. Why wouldn't he?

"Fitzgerald always amazes me," my mom said, looping her arm into my dad's as they followed Kevin through the double doors.

I turned to my crew—Kiesha, Lola, Lila, and of course, Nola. "Y'all ready?"

Nola smirked. "Let's go. Let's embrace the new."

Inside was like stepping into the pages of Architectural Digest—faith edition.

Floor-to-ceiling windows poured sunlight across sleek marble floors. Velvet furniture wrapped in gold accents made the rooms feel royal but cozy. Every detail whispered intention. And despite the elegance, there was warmth. A lived-in, loved-in feel.

As we walked past the formal living room, family lounge, and a massive dining area, we entered a space where Fitzgerald stood waiting.

And whew, Lord—my man looked like favor in human form.

The way he smiled when he saw me?

I forgot how to blink.

"**Welcome home, family,**" he said, his voice calm and strong. "**Miera, I wanted everyone to experience this with you. This is just the beginning.**"

Brother Kevin passed out glasses of sparkling cider and champagne while Fitz gave a short toast. I couldn't even process the words—I was too busy watching him. Watching the life I prayed for unfold in real time.

We climbed to the **second level**, and Fitzgerald paused at the end of the hallway where seven doors lined the corridor.

Two doors stood out—each with an ornate gold crown on them. One marked with a **K**, the other with a **Q**.

"This one," Fitz said, motioning to the *K*, "is your room, my princess. Soon to be queen."

He and my dad stepped aside for a quiet conversation while my sisters swarmed me like curious bees.

Nola, of course, spoke first. "**Wait a minute. So y'all live in this massive love castle... and you got separate rooms? What is this—The Virgin Diaries?!**"

Lola and Lila chimed in.

"Yeah, that's mad weird," Lola muttered. "Ain't y'all grown?"

Before I could clap back, my mom stepped forward like the graceful powerhouse she is.

"Ladies," she said, voice soft but solid, "**this is one of the most romantic things a man can do.** Your sister is being honored. He's choosing to wait. That's not weak—that's *power*."

Then she turned to me. "Miera, talk to him. Make sure it aligns with your heart and your walk with God. If it does, trust his leadership. Because soon... you'll be walking together."

"Thanks, Mama," I whispered, resting in her arms for a moment—just a daughter soaking in her mother's covering.

Fitzgerald and Daddy rejoined the group, laughing like old best friends.

"What'd we miss?" Fitz asked with a grin.

"Oh, just a little curiosity about the whole 'no sleepovers' situation," Nola said, crossing her arms like an FBI agent.

Fitz chuckled. "I figured y'all would notice that."

My dad clapped him on the back. "Told you—this crew doesn't miss a thing."

Fitz turned to Nola. "Since the day I met y'all on that bus, I knew you were gonna be the one to keep Miera on her toes. And clearly... you got me on mine too."

Then he addressed the whole group.

"**I chose to sleep in a separate room because I want to honor Miera and our commitment to God.** I know what we share is real. And I don't want to taint it. I want to build it *right*. After we're married? It's on. But until then? She's my princess—and I'll treat her like one."

Nola's jaw dropped. **"Dang, Fitz! Do you got any saved and sanctified brothers who look like that? 'Cause I'm tryna build the kingdom too!"**

We all *busted out laughing.*

"Girl, bye," I said, shaking my head. "You play too much."

But inside, my heart whispered:

God, you did that.

Late That Night...

The house was quiet now.

The laughter had faded.
The champagne glasses were washed.
The last hug had been given.

My family was gone. My friends had gone home.
And I was... alone.

In my new room—**the "Q" room**—I sat at the edge of a velvet cream chaise lounge, wrapped in one of the softest robes I'd ever worn. My overnight bag sat unopened in the corner. I hadn't even changed. I just needed a moment to sit. To breathe.

The silence felt thick. Almost sacred.

All around me was beauty—gold finishes, warm lighting, and the faint scent of peonies from a vase by the window. But inside? I felt this slow, quiet ache that I couldn't quite explain.

Why do new blessings sometimes feel so heavy?

I walked over to the window and looked out over the city. The skyline twinkled in the distance, and the moon hung like a promise just waiting to be fulfilled.

"God," I whispered, "what do I do with all this?"

I wasn't doubting the blessing. I wasn't second-guessing the love.
But this was... *big*. Bigger than anything I'd ever known.
And for the first time, I felt the weight of becoming.

Becoming a woman.
Becoming a wife.
Becoming who I said I always wanted to be.

I sat on the bed, pulled my journal from my nightstand drawer, and opened to a blank page. I didn't have the words yet—but I needed to start.

"Dear Future Me," I wrote.
"Don't forget how this moment feels..."

Tears began to fall—quietly. Not sad tears. Not fearful ones.
Just... a soft release.
Like my soul was exhaling after holding its breath for years.

I thought of **my mom**, and how she smiled through the entire tour with tears hiding behind her lashes.

I thought of **my dad**, and how he gave Fitzgerald that firm handshake—the kind that said "Take care of my girl, or else."

I thought of **Nola**, always loud, always loyal—who never let me forget that I was worth friendship, even when the world said I wasn't.

And I thought of **Fitzgerald**, who walked me through the house like a man who knew he had found his favor—and didn't take that lightly.

A knock came at the door—soft and respectful.

I wiped my tears and called, "Come in."

Fitz stood there, barefoot, dressed in black joggers and a white tee, holding a warm cup of tea.

"Chamomile," he said, holding it out. "You always say it helps you sleep."

I smiled as I took it from him.

He stepped back, careful not to cross the invisible line he promised to honor.

"You good?" he asked softly.

I nodded. "Just... processing."

He paused. "Me too."

I looked at him—really looked at him—and saw the man God handpicked for me. Not perfect. But intentional. Purposeful. And chosen.

"I love you, Miera," he said. "Not for what you do or how you look. I love the way you love God. The way you carry your family. The way you still get overwhelmed and try to hide it. You're strong... and tender. And I promise to keep loving every piece of you as you evolve."

I blinked back fresh tears. "I love you too. Thank you for giving me space to be human."

He smiled. "Always. I'll let you rest."

He started to leave, then paused. "I know this is a lot. But just remember—you don't have to embrace it all in one night. One breath at a time, baby."

And with that, he quietly closed the door.

I sat there for a while, sipping my tea, staring at the door he just walked through. And then I whispered again:

"God... I can do this. Not because I'm strong—but because You're with me."

I crawled into bed, pulled the covers up to my chin, and let peace do what peace does best.

Settle me.
Hold me.
Prepare me.

Tomorrow will come. The journey would continue.
But tonight?
I rested. Whole. Loved. Becoming.

Chapter 5: This Is Different

"Therefore, if anyone is in Christ, the new creation has come: The old has gone, the new is here!"

– 2 Corinthians 5:17

The house was quiet.

Too quiet.

After all the laughter, the ooh's and ahh's, the selfies in the marble bathroom, and the ten-minute debate over who was riding back with whom—it was just me.

Alone in my room.

My room.

The moonlight spilled through the tall windows, brushing across the plush bedding and glinting off the gold trim on my mirror. I stood there in my robe, barefoot on the heated floor, still not believing all this was mine.

I walked over to the vanity and sat down, brushing out my hair slowly, trying to process the whirlwind of the day.

My sisters were gone. My parents were gone. Nola was gone.

And Fitzgerald...

He texted not long ago:

"Let me know once you've showered and settled. I'm not done loving on you yet."

I smiled at my phone.

Just as I slid under the silk sheets, there was a soft knock at my door.

I sat up.

"Come in," I called, assuming it was one of the house staff bringing tea or a late-night something.

But it was him.

Fitzgerald stepped inside, dressed in all black—suit tailored, cologne bold but soft, that look on his face that told me he was up to something.

"Why are you dressed like a midnight miracle?" I asked, squinting at him.

He chuckled and walked over, pulling me gently from the bed.

"I know you're winding down, but I need five minutes. Can I steal you for just five?" he said, holding both my hands.

"Fitz... it's late," I said with a groan, although I was already grabbing my robe tighter and standing up.

"It's never too late to create a core memory," he whispered, brushing my cheek. "Come downstairs with me."

We padded softly down the curved staircase, my bare feet quiet against the steps. As we reached the main level, soft lighting lit the space, and music played faintly in the background—**Major's "Why I Love You."**

I turned to him slowly.

"What is this?"

Fitzgerald opened the front door.

Outside was a black luxury Sprinter van—and standing beside it was my father.

And my mother.

And my sisters.

And Nola.

"What in the—"

"We didn't go far," my mom said, smiling, eyes twinkling. "He told us to give you your moment... and then come back."

Fitzgerald turned to my dad. "Sir, if it's alright with you..."

My dad grinned, already knowing what was about to happen. "Son, take it away."

Fitz took a deep breath, then turned to me.

"Miera Nielsen," he began. "Today marked a new beginning. You stepped into a house built just for you... for us. But before life takes off and the next chapter begins, I want to give you and your family one more core memory. One that says: 'You did it.' One that says: 'You are surrounded by love.' One that reminds you that your joy is worth pausing for."

He took my hand again.

"If it's alright with you," he said, locking eyes with me, "I'd like to fly all of us to Paris tonight. Dinner cruise. Seine River. Private chef. Live music. Laughter. Light. Love."

I stood frozen.

"... *Tonight?*" I barely whispered.

He nodded.

"The jet is ready. Bags are already packed. I figured if we're going to celebrate the new... let's do it with style."

For a full ten seconds, I just stared at him.

Then Nola screamed, "*Girl if you don't say something, I will!*"

The entire group erupted into laughter. My dad was already loading the van, my mom dabbing her eyes, and my sisters trying to grab their "Paris Face" makeup bags.

I looked back at Fitz—still standing calm and confident, waiting for my reaction.

And all I could say was:

"Fitzgerald... this is different."

He leaned in, kissed my forehead, and whispered:

"That's because *you're* different."

We loaded into the Sprinter, buzzing with disbelief and excitement.

"Who even does stuff like this?" Lola whispered to Lila.

"I don't know, but I'm claiming it for my life," Lila whispered back, pulling out her journal to start writing affirmations.

I slid into a seat near the window, watching the night blur past as we headed to Jet Linx. Fitzgerald sat beside me, fingers laced through mine.

"You good?" he asked, voice low and smooth.

"I don't even know what I am," I said honestly. "Overwhelmed. Happy. Light Headed. Slightly suspicious, this is a dream."

He laughed. "You'll believe it when you're sipping sparkling water with lemon on a Parisian yacht."

"Or when Nola starts crying because her lashes froze," I said, grinning.

"You know she already packed extra glue just in case."

When we pulled up to the private hangar, I lost it.

The jet wasn't just "ready"—it was glowing. White exterior, name etched in gold near the door: *The Nielsen Flight.*

"Wait a minute…" I turned to him slowly. "You named the jet?"

"Correction," he said, smirking. "**Our** jet."

Everybody screamed like we were headed to The Grammys.

As we boarded, plush white leather seats, warm lights, and glass flutes of sparkling juice greeted us. My mom clutched her pearls. My dad leaned back like he had always belonged here.

The flight was smooth and filled with joy.

We laughed. Took photos. Nola turned the aisle into a runway. My sisters played UNO like they were on a mission from heaven. My dad read Psalms. My mom kept asking for the steward's skincare routine. Fitzgerald wrapped me in his arms under a blanket, whispering random questions:

"If I were a dessert, what would I be?"

I turned to him with a smirk. "Sweet potato pie. Smooth. Satisfying. Unexpectedly addictive."

He laughed, eyes twinkling. "Then you're strawberry shortcake. Sweet, layered, and everybody wants a slice."

"Fitzgerald!"

"What?" he shrugged. "Tell me I'm lying."

We landed in Paris just before sunrise.

The Eiffel Tower was glowing like a promise. The air was cool and crisp, wrapping around us like silk. A black Mercedes convoy awaited us with a guide holding a sign that read: *Welcome, The Future Mr. & Mrs.*

Fitz leaned in. "You ready?"

"I'm still trying to catch up," I said, blinking through the beauty.

The river cruise was *next-level romantic*.

Glass ceilings. Floating chandeliers. Candlelit tables with rose petals. A string quartet playing everything from Sade to Lauryn Hill. Waiters with accents smoother than Fitzgerald's suit.

As we floated along the Seine, past cathedrals and centuries-old bridges, my mom toasted with tears in her eyes. My sisters giggled over the menu, confused but adventurous. My dad looked at me like I was still his baby girl, but now someone else's queen too.

Fitz pulled out my chair, sat beside me, and held my hand under the table. "Look around," he whispered. "This is what love looks like. Community. Celebration. Peace."

"You did this," I whispered back.

"No," he said, shaking his head. "**God did this.** I just obeyed the blueprint."

As dessert arrived—chocolate soufflé and gold-dusted strawberries—the quartet shifted tunes.

Major's *"Why I Love You"* again.

Fitz turned to me, eyes locking on mine. "Miera," he said, "I don't know what tomorrow holds, but I promise to keep making today beautiful."

"I don't need perfection," I whispered.

"Good," he said, smiling, "because I ain't perfect. But I'm yours."

The boat rocked gently. Paris sparkled behind us. And in that moment?

I stopped asking if this was too good to be true.

Because this wasn't a fairy tale.

It was *favor*.

And I was finally learning how to receive it.

Morning After: Stillness & Sunrise

The next morning, sunlight spilled through the sheer Parisian curtains like it had been sent on assignment. Warm, golden light danced across the plush bedding, kissing the tops of my shoulders and gently pulling me from sleep.

I blinked, stretched, and rolled over...

Fitzgerald wasn't there.

I sat up, the oversized robe slipping off my shoulder, and looked around the suite—high ceilings, crown molding, gold-trimmed mirrors. The kind of room that made you feel like royalty just for breathing.

I found a handwritten note on the pillow beside me.

> **"Didn't want to wake you—your peace was too beautiful.**
> **Meet me on the rooftop when you're ready.**
> **There's coffee, croissants, and a view that doesn't compare to you... but I tried.**
> **—Mr. Wonderful"**

I smiled so hard my cheeks hurt.

After a quick shower, I slipped into a soft ivory jumpsuit and light sandals, tied my curls up into a puff, and made my way to the rooftop.

The elevator opened to a warm breeze and the smell of strong espresso. I stepped out to find Fitzgerald standing near the ledge, looking out over the city like he owned it—or maybe just like he belonged to it.

"Hey you," I called out softly.

He turned and smiled. "There she is—*Madame Magic.*"

I raised an eyebrow. "Is that what we're going with now?"

"Absolutely. You made last night feel enchanted. You're the magic."

He pulled out my chair and poured me a fresh cup. I took a sip, closed my eyes, and let the moment melt into my bones.

"So," he said, watching me closely, "was it worth it?"

I didn't answer right away.

Instead, I looked around—at the view, the quiet, the calm after the celebration.

And then I looked at him.

"The old me would've questioned it to death," I said. "Wondered what it would cost. Looked for the strings attached. Braced for the fall."

He reached for my hand.

"But the woman I'm becoming?" I continued. "She receives. She believes. And she knows this kind of love doesn't just happen. It's intentional. It's heaven-approved."

His eyes welled slightly, but he blinked it back.

"Thank you for letting me love you this way," he said. "It's never been about doing the most—it's about giving you what you deserve, and showing your people they deserve it too."

"You've already done that, Fitz," I whispered. "You didn't just show up. You covered, you created, you honored. That's rare."

He stood, walked over, and kissed my forehead.

"I plan to be rare for the rest of our lives."

I leaned into him, heart full.

We didn't say much after that. We didn't need to.

The city of love pulsed beneath us. The sky blushed. The breeze wrapped around us like God's hand.

It was quiet.

It was simple.

It was sacred.

And for the first time in a long time...

I didn't feel like I had to prove anything.

I could just *be*.

Touching down in Chicago felt like returning to the familiar—but this time, we weren't going *home* the way we used to.

Our driver met us on the tarmac and quickly loaded our things into a black luxury shuttle. No pit stops. No delays. Just us, riding in peaceful silence, still floating from the beauty of Paris.

As the sun began to rise, we pulled into **OakBrook**—an upscale suburb just outside of Chicago, where everything felt polished, peaceful, and private. The tree-lined streets curved like pages in a storybook, and the air held that fresh, rich glow of new beginnings.

When the gates to our estate opened and the familiar winding driveway came into view, everyone quietly took it in.

"This still doesn't feel real," Lola said, adjusting her bonnet like she was seeing it for the first time.

"I feel like I'm in one of those Hallmark movies," Nola added. "Except the budget is bigger, and the main character got hips."

We all laughed—even though we were barely awake.

Fitzgerald helped everyone out of the shuttle and gave instructions to the staff while we dragged our overnight bags inside. The chef had a breakfast spread waiting—fluffy croissants, fresh fruit, crispy turkey bacon, and eggs with cheese just the way we liked.

It was our last meal together before the family would head back to the South Side.

We sat around the oversized kitchen island, still dressed in our airport clothes, laughing between bites and retelling Paris highlights like we hadn't all lived the same memories.

"I still can't believe y'all had a full violin section playing 'Before I Let Go' on the river," Kiesha said.

"And Fitzgerald clinking glasses with Daddy like they've been best friends since grammar school," Lila added, giggling.

My dad smiled proudly. "That's my son now. Y'all better get used to it."

After breakfast, my sisters helped me unpack while my parents walked the property one last time. There was an unspoken stillness in the air—like we all knew this was the end of something... and the beginning of everything else.

As they gathered their things, my mom hugged me tight, her voice calm but full of wisdom. "You were built for this. Just don't lose *you* in it."

My dad kissed my forehead. "Call me if you sneeze twice, okay?"

"Y'all act like I'm not gonna see you in a week," I teased, blinking away tears.

"We know," Lola said. "But this is still major."

And it was.

I stood at the door and waved until the shuttle disappeared behind the gates.

Then I turned around—and felt the full weight of the quiet.

This house, so full of joy just an hour ago, was now... still. Silent.

Fitzgerald came up behind me, wrapped his arms around my waist, and rested his chin on my shoulder.

"You good, baby?" he whispered.

I nodded. "Just taking it in."

"New beginnings," he said. "This house... this chapter... it's all yours."

I smiled. "Ours."

But as I looked out at the driveway, where the shuttle had vanished... something in me whispered:

Things are about to change.

Chapter 6: Things Get Interesting

"It is the glory of God to conceal a matter; to search out a matter is the glory of kings."

-Proverbs 25:2

The mansion felt like a different world without the laughter of my sisters echoing through the halls or my dad's random outbursts about snacks missing from the pantry.

The family had only been gone a few hours, but the silence? It was loud.

I stood in the grand foyer, still barefoot, still in my pajamas, watching the sunlight stream in through the floor-to-ceiling windows. Everything looked picture perfect—still glowing with the magic of Paris, the trunk party, and all the extravagant firsts. But deep down, I felt something shifting.

Fitzgerald was already on the move—some call, some errand, some appointment. He kissed me on the forehead and whispered, "Rest, baby. I'll be back in a few."

That should've comforted me. But instead, I just nodded and smiled like everything was fine.

After a long, hot shower and slipping into one of his oversized hoodies, I curled up in the plush armchair near the window in my room. I tried journaling. Tried reading. Tried watching a sermon.

But something inside wouldn't settle.

The way Fitzgerald had been moving lately—it was still loving, still intentional—but there were moments when it felt like he was hiding something. Nothing obvious. Just... subtle things. Late-night phone calls. Vague answers. Locked doors I never noticed before.

I finally fell asleep mid-thought.

That night, I woke up around 2:14 a.m.—heart racing, skin prickled like something had pulled me out of sleep.

I heard voices. Low. Muffled.

I slipped out of bed and tiptoed down the hall, drawn to the sound like something inside me *needed* to know.

Fitzgerald's door was cracked.

"I don't care what it costs. Just make sure everything is ready by next week," he said, voice firm but restrained.

"You know this could complicate things," another man replied.

I didn't recognize the voice. Something about it made my stomach knot.

"It'll be fine," Fitz said. "I've got it under control."

My heart dropped into my gut.

I backed away from the door slowly, careful not to make a sound, and tiptoed back to my room. I slid under the covers like a child hiding from a nightmare.

What is he planning? And why the secrecy?

The next morning, the house looked exactly the same.

Bright. Lavish. Full of peace.

But *I* wasn't.

We sat down for breakfast. Fitz was charming, attentive, cracking jokes like normal—but behind those warm eyes, I saw flickers of something else. Something I couldn't read.

"You okay, baby?" he asked, watching me stir my tea without taking a sip.

"Yeah," I said with a smile that didn't quite reach my soul. "Just still tired from the trip."

He nodded. "I figured. We've got a big week coming up. Rest if you need to."

I watched him carefully, wondering what exactly this "big week" entailed.

Later that day, after the house had quieted and Fitzgerald was gone again, I found myself exploring the hallways like it was my first time there.

That's when I noticed a door I hadn't seen before.

Tucked at the end of a corridor, behind a decorative panel that almost blended into the wall.

I turned the knob.

Locked.

"What are you doing?"

I jumped. Fitzgerald was behind me—quiet, unreadable, perfectly still.

"Just exploring," I said, hoping my voice didn't give me away.

He smiled. But it didn't quite reach his eyes. "Some doors are better left closed, Miera."

My chest tightened as he turned and walked away.

That was the moment I knew:

My new life may have come wrapped in luxury and love...

But it also came with **layers**.

And I was going to uncover every single one of them.

Even if it meant pulling the thread that unraveled everything.

Chapter 7: Woman's Intuition

"The human spirit is the lamp of the Lord that sheds light on one's inmost being."
-**Proverbs 20:27**

The door shouldn't have mattered.

It was just wood and paint, hinges and a handle. But every time Miera passed it, her pace slowed. Her breath caught. Her thoughts spiraled.

There was something about it.

Not just the way it seemed to blend into the wall—hidden in plain sight—but the way her spirit reacted. Like it *knew*. Like it remembered something her mind hadn't been told yet.

She tried to shake it off.

Tried to focus on school prep, on unpacking, on getting to know the rhythm of her new life.

But that door? It was always there.

Watching. Waiting.

Even when she wasn't looking at it, it lived in the back of her mind.

Fitzgerald noticed. He was attentive, as always—but a little more guarded. He brought her breakfast in bed. He lit candles when she bathed. He even left sticky notes around the house with little affirmations:

"You're seen. You're safe. You're mine."
  –Fitz

But he also changed the subject whenever she got too curious. And that? That was new.

One night, as they sat watching TV on the oversized couch, she turned to him.

"Fitz... can I ask you something?"

He muted the TV and gave her his full attention. "Of course."

"That door down the hall," she said slowly. "Why is it locked?"

He didn't flinch. But his jaw flexed—just for a second. Just enough for her to catch.

"It's not important," he said gently. "Just a storage space I haven't gotten around to cleaning."

She nodded slowly but didn't press. Her intuition whispered, *Lie.*

Fitz reached for her hand. "You trust me, right?"

"Yes," she replied.

But it came out too fast.

Too light.

Even she didn't believe it.

That night, Miera lay awake longer than usual. Her body was exhausted, but her mind raced. The dream returned—the same one she'd had since the night she first saw the door.

Darkness. A whisper. A child's voice. Then silence.

The next morning, she rose before the sun. The house was still, silent except for the distant hum of appliances.

Barefoot, she crept toward the hallway.

The door waited.

She reached out.

Still locked.

"Looking for something?" Fitzgerald's voice floated from behind her like smoke.

She jumped, spinning to face him. His eyes weren't cold—but they weren't warm, either.

Just... unreadable.

"Just exploring again," she said, wrapping her arms around herself.

"You've been restless," he said. "I see it in your eyes. You don't have to be."

He stepped closer. Close enough for her to feel the heat of his chest, but not enough to touch.

"You think I'm hiding something," he said, voice low. "And maybe I am. But not because I want to hurt you. Some truths don't come with timing—they come with weight. And when you carry weight too early, it crushes you."

He stepped forward, brushed a curl from her face.

"When I open that door, it won't be because you knocked loud enough. It'll be because I know you're ready to hold what's on the other side."

Miera's heart pounded.

"But Fitz—how will I know it's not just my curiosity... or fear?"

He smiled, soft but sad. "You'll know because your spirit won't scream anymore."

He kissed her forehead and turned away, leaving her in the hallway, alone with her questions.

And for the first time, Miera didn't want the answers all at once.

She just wanted the truth.

Even if it shattered everything else.

Chapter 8: Suspense Builds

"Call to me and I will answer you and tell you great and unsearchable things you do not know."

-Jeremiah 33:3

They began their morning in silence, moving in an unspoken rhythm down the hallway toward the door. The air was thicker today—charged with tension and curiosity. Miera's eyes scanned every inch of the corridor for signs of a key—under rugs, behind picture frames, even tucked into the ornate molding along the wall. Fitzgerald searched too, but something about his calm demeanor made her pause.

He wasn't frustrated. He wasn't intrigued.

He was controlled.

Calculated.

Her eyes narrowed slightly. He knew something. She could feel it. It was in the way his jaw tightened when her fingers brushed the doorknob again. The way he avoided meeting her eyes whenever she asked a direct question.

"You've been in this house longer than I have," she said casually. "Are you sure you've never seen a key for this door?"

"Not that I can remember. I never had a reason to look for one," he answered smoothly.

But it felt rehearsed.

The seed of suspicion bloomed inside her. Was he protecting her? Or hiding something from her?

Before her thoughts could spiral too far, a voice broke the silence.

"It's not the key you need. It's permission."

They turned.

Standing at the end of the hallway was Ms. Eloise—their next-door neighbor. The woman was small in frame, but her presence filled the space like thunder before a storm. Her eyes held wisdom. And a warning.

"Excuse me?" Miera asked.

Ms. Eloise stepped forward slowly, her cane tapping against the floor. "That door wasn't locked by accident. It's not just keeping something in—it's keeping you from something until you're ready."

Fitzgerald stiffened beside her.

"What's behind it?" Miera's voice was quiet, but her heart thundered in her chest.

Ms. Eloise tilted her head. "Memories. Pain. Truth. Maybe even a little magic. But most of all... answers. Ones you may not be ready for."

"Then why are you telling me now?" Miera asked.

"Because now... you're asking the right questions."

With that, Ms. Eloise turned and walked away, leaving behind more weight than clarity.

Miera stood frozen. Fitzgerald gently reached for her, pulling her in close. His hands found her waist, grounding her. "Breathe, baby," he whispered, his voice soft against the noise in her head. "Don't go so deep in your mind that you miss what's right in front of you. I'm here. I've always been here."

His presence calmed her. His lips brushed her temple, then drifted to her jawline. That touch—intentional, warm, reverent—made her breath hitch.

A soft moan slipped from her lips.

Fitzgerald pulled back slightly, eyes searching hers. "You okay?"

"I am now," she whispered, fingers curling around the fabric of his shirt. "But if you keep touching me like that, we're not making it to the door today."

He smiled, tension melting away.

"Maybe that's not such a bad thing."

His lips found hers again—slower this time, deeper. Clothes slipped away between shared breaths and gentle sighs. They moved together, wrapped in longing and love, in heat and hunger.

But just as he touched the inside of her thigh—

A lightning bolt of clarity struck.

The door.

The secrets.

Her past.

Her breath caught—not in pleasure this time, but panic.

Fitzgerald paused when he felt her go still. He looked into her eyes and saw it: the shift.

"What's wrong?"

She stared up at the ceiling, eyes glassy. "I need a minute."

He moved back gently, covering her with a throw blanket. "Talk to me."

Miera sat up, wrapping the blanket around her like armor. "I thought I was ready. I wanted to be. But something about this moment triggered me."

He listened without interruption.

"In the past... giving myself like that, too soon, always left me broken. Sex became an escape—but it always left me more empty than before. I've grown. I've healed. I made a vow to God. And I want to honor that—even now."

He took her hand. "But you want you more."

She looked at him, stunned. "Exactly."

Fitzgerald leaned his forehead against hers. "Then we slow down. We don't rush our love, our story, or the opening of that door. What's for us will meet us at the pace of purpose."

Tears fell from her eyes, but they weren't from shame. They were release.

"I'm sorry," she whispered.

"Don't be," he said. "Real love waits."

And in the sacred silence that followed, Miera leaned into him. Not for escape. But for safety. For surrender without compromise.

She wasn't running anymore.

She was rising.

The door could wait.

But her healing?

It had just begun.

Chapter 9: The Uneasy Truth

"Therefore each of you must put off falsehood and speak truthfully to your neighbor, for we are all members of one body."
-Ephesians 4:25

The morning sun was doing its best to convince the world it was a brand-new day—but Miera wasn't buying it. She sat in bed, legs curled under her, robe tied tight like armor. Her body had rested, but her spirit had not.

The echo of last night lingered in the air like perfume—sweet, heated, intimate... until the moment broke. That door had snuck into her spirit like a thief. And now? It was all she could think about.

She stepped into the hallway barefoot, every step drawing her back to *that* spot. The door. The secret. The silence.

But before she could even reach it, she heard footsteps—and then his voice.

"You're up early," Fitzgerald said, leaning against the wall. He was shirtless, glistening from a fresh run, towel around his neck. The man was fine. Like... disrespectfully fine. And that only irritated her more.

"I couldn't sleep," she said, voice clipped.

He walked toward her with that smooth, effortless confidence that used to make her melt. "Is it... the door again?"

That did it.

She turned, arms folded. "You say that like it's an annoying dream I can't shake. But let's be real, Fitz—why do *you* keep dancing around it?"

He paused. Just for a second. But that hesitation told her everything.

"Miera..." he started.

"No," she cut in. "You've been playing calm. Acting clueless. But I feel it. You *know* something. And every time I get close, you gaslight me into thinking I'm crazy."

He looked away. "It's not that simple."

"Then make it simple!" she snapped. "What's behind that door?"

Before he could answer, the doorbell rang.

Saved by the bell. Or maybe... damned by it.

"I'll get it," he said quickly, disappearing down the hall.

Miera stayed frozen. Her nerves were dancing in her chest.

Then she heard her.

A woman's voice.

"Hi. Sorry to pop up like this... is Fitzgerald home?"

Who?

Her blood turned cold.

"Jasmin?" Fitzgerald's voice carried down the hall—soft, familiar.

Miera's feet moved before her mind caught up. She stepped around the corner and stopped cold.

And there she was.

Jasmin.

The kind of beautiful that walked in like a memory you never deleted. Glowing brown skin. Jet-black hair slicked into a high ponytail. Designer bag hanging from her arm. And confidence? On a hundred.

Miera's mouth opened before she could filter the rage. "Fitz, who is *she*?"

Fitz turned, jaw tight. "This is Jasmin."

Jasmin offered a polite smile that felt like a dagger. "You didn't tell her?"

"Tell me *what*?" Miera demanded.

Jasmin stepped in farther—too comfortable. Too familiar.

"I used to live here," she said. "With him."

The world tilted.

"I'm his ex-fiancée."

Silence.

Fitzgerald's face was unreadable. But Miera felt like she'd just been punched in the soul.

"You what?" she whispered.

"It was before you," Fitz said quickly, stepping forward. "A year ago. It's over."

"But you *never* said anything. You let me move into a house you shared with another woman—like it was a clean slate? Like this wasn't sacred ground already tainted?"

"Miera—"

"No," she said, tears stinging the edges of her eyes. "You knew how much transparency mattered to me. And you kept *this* from me?"

"It wasn't like that," he said, reaching for her.

"You didn't *lie*, Fitz?" she snapped, voice rising. "You just conveniently didn't mention your ex lived here, slept here, probably made love to you in the same bed—"

"Stop," he said, quietly. "Please."

The shame in his eyes was real. But so was the betrayal burning in her chest.

Then Jasmin spoke again, cool as ice. "I left something here. Behind that locked door."

Miera turned sharply. "*What?*"

Jasmin shrugged. "We used to keep... things behind it. Sentimental stuff. I figured he would've told you."

Miera's heart dropped.

She looked at Fitzgerald like she didn't know him anymore. "You said you didn't know what was behind that door."

"I was trying to protect you," he said, his voice heavy.

She backed up slowly, her voice cracking like glass. "No, Fitz. You were protecting *yourself.*"

The silence that followed didn't just fill the room—it stabbed it.

Fitzgerald looked down, guilt written all over him.

Jasmin looked like she'd gotten the closure she came for.

And Miera?

She stood there, robe tight around her, heart ripped open, staring down the hallway like the house itself had betrayed her.

The door wasn't just hiding secrets.

It had just opened one.

And now she had a choice to make: retreat... or face what else might be waiting on the other side.

Chapter 10: When Silence Screams Loudest

"The Lord is close to the brokenhearted and saves those who are crushed in spirit."
-Psalm 34:18

Miera didn't scream.

She didn't shout.

She didn't slap him, even though her palms itched to.

She just... moved.

Past Fitzgerald.

Past Jasmin.

Past every dream she had wrapped in this man's mouth.

And straight out the front door.

The slam behind her was soft, but it thundered through her soul like a final bell. Her breath caught in her throat as the sunlight smacked her skin like a slap from reality. She didn't know where she was going. She didn't care.

She just needed to get away from the lie wearing a tailored suit and a cologne she still loved.

By the time she got in the car, her hands were shaking. Her heart was beating like it was trying to outrun the betrayal—and losing. She turned the key. No music. No GPS. Just her and the war inside her chest.

The mansion—the love story—the "God wrote this" fairytale—was behind her.

And it was burning.

Not with fire. But with truth.
And truth doesn't need flames to burn down your whole world.

She drove.
Tears didn't fall. Not yet.
But something inside her cracked with every mile.

God... did I choose this? Or did You?
And if You did... Why does it hurt like hell?

When she pulled up to her parents' house, the front porch light flicked on like Heaven itself had been waiting. She hadn't called. Hadn't texted. But somehow, her mama knew.

Because before she could even grab her keys or fix her face, the door flew open.

"Mama..." she whispered.
And then her knees buckled.

Her mother caught her mid-collapse, arms strong, voice soft but sure.
"I felt it in my spirit. Come on in, baby. You're safe now."

She didn't speak another word.

Not until she hit the floor in the prayer room—her sanctuary since childhood.
The scent of anointing oil and the soft hum of gospel in the background pulled her into a sacred hush.

She dropped to her knees and *wailed*.

"God…" Her voice cracked open. "I trusted him. I trusted You! I prayed. I fasted. I gave You my yes. Why does it feel like You gave me a 'no' in return?"

Her fists hit the carpet. Her robe tangled around her as she bowed so low her forehead hit the floor.

"I was ready for love. For legacy. For forever. I *wanted* this. I thought You *sent* this."
She looked up, her voice hoarse. "Was I blind? Or did I just believe too hard?"

She opened the Bible, needing something—anything. And like fire, it landed on:

"The Lord is close to the brokenhearted and saves those who are crushed in spirit."
—Psalm 34:18

Her breath hitched.
Her heart cracked wider.
And finally… the tears came.

"God, I don't want this pain to become poison. I don't want this disappointment to rewrite my identity. I don't want this man's mistake to make me forget who *You* said I am."

She opened again.
This time:

"He heals the brokenhearted and binds up their wounds."
—Psalm 147:3

"Yes, Lord. Bind mine. Because right now, I'm bleeding everywhere."

One more flip.

Another whisper from Heaven:

"Be still and know that I am God."
—Psalm 46:10

She let out a shaky exhale, arms limp now. The storm inside was still raging—but something in her shifted. A quiet resolve. A fire reignited under the ashes.

"If it's not from You, burn it, God. Burn every lie. Every hidden room. Every ghost of a love that was never real. And if somehow it *is* from You, redeem it. Rebuild it brick by brick. But I won't rescue what You're trying to remove."

She stayed in that posture of prayer until her knees throbbed and her soul exhaled.

And then...

She rose.

Not because the pain was gone.

But because the *power* had returned.

When she stepped out of the prayer room, her mama had her favorite tea waiting and the couch fluffed like a throne.

"Rest now, baby," she said. "No explaining. Just healing."

Miera curled up, clutching the warm mug with trembling fingers.

And in the silence that followed, God didn't shout.

He whispered.

"This isn't the end. This is the exposure before elevation."

Chapter 11: When Grace Feels Like a Mountain

"Come to me, all you who are weary and burdened, and I will give you rest. Take my yoke upon you and learn from me, for I am gentle and humble in heart, and you will find rest for your souls. For my yoke is easy and my burden is light."

-Matthew 11:28-30

The sun peeked through the living room curtains as Miera lay still under her mother's blanket. She hadn't slept much—her body had rested, but her spirit was restless. She stared at the ceiling, wondering how love could taste so sweet one moment and feel like betrayal the next.

The weight of the previous day was still draped over her like a fog. Her mind replayed everything—the locked door, Jasmin's confident entrance, Fitzgerald's hesitation, the half-truths. It wasn't just the situation that broke her. It was the silence. The omission. The knowing and not telling.

But what stunned her even more than Fitzgerald's past was the mirror it held up to her own.

She sat up slowly, her hands gripping the edge of the blanket. "God... I feel like I'm spiraling."

Her Bible from the night before was still open on the coffee table. She pulled it into her lap, fingers trembling. "I want to forgive, but I don't even know where to begin."

As she flipped through the pages, tears already rising, her eyes landed on:

"Get rid of all bitterness, rage and anger... forgiving each other, just as in Christ God forgave you."
— *Ephesians 4:31-32*

She exhaled shakily. "But God... how do I forgive someone who shattered my trust?"

She closed her eyes—and that's when the memories came rushing back.

Before Fitzgerald, there was another. A boy she thought would be her forever. The one who introduced her to heartbreak and manipulation under the guise of love. She gave him everything—her time, her body, her dreams. And in return, he gave her lies, infidelity, and wounds she thought she buried years ago.

She never told Fitzgerald about him. Never shared how that boy's betrayal planted a seed of doubt so deep, it sometimes still whispered that she wasn't enough.

"God," she whispered, "maybe this is the root. Maybe I'm reacting now because I never healed then."

She turned to another page, her eyes catching:

"He heals the brokenhearted and binds up their wounds."
— *Psalm 147:3*

And then:

"Trust in the Lord with all your heart and lean not on your own understanding."
— *Proverbs 3:5*

It wasn't just about Fitzgerald. It was about every unhealed version of herself screaming out from the past.

She placed her hand on her chest. "Help me not to bleed on someone who didn't cause the wound."

She flipped again.

"Above all, love each other deeply, because love covers over a multitude of sins."
— *1 Peter 4:8*

And finally:

"If you forgive other people when they sin against you, your heavenly Father will also forgive you."
— *Matthew 6:14*

Her heart ached, but it also softened. Forgiveness wasn't about excusing the past—it was about freeing her future.

She took a deep breath, whispered into the stillness, "Okay, God... I'm willing to rebuild. Brick by brick. Heart first."

The sun had long shifted across the sky by the time Miera emerged from the prayer room. Her spirit was steadier now, but her heart still pulsed with questions. She made her way to the kitchen where her mom stood silently preparing tea like she already knew what was stirring in her daughter's chest.

"Come sit, baby," her mama said without turning around.

Miera eased into the chair, hands folded in her lap. Her voice came out barely above a whisper. "Mama, what if I can't trust him again?"

Her mother placed the tea in front of her and sat across the table. "Trust don't rebuild itself, baby. It's laid one brick at a time. And every brick gotta be placed with truth, grace, and time."

"I feel like a fool," Miera confessed. "Like I wanted it so bad to be God that I ignored the whispers."

Her mama tilted her head. "Or maybe... you were just hoping the whispers weren't warning signs. That's not foolish—that's human. But this?" She tapped the table gently. "This is where you listen again."

Miera sighed, tears returning. "He says he wants to be better—with me, not just for me. He admitted his mistake. He sounded... sincere."

"Then ask yourself this," her mother said. "Do you want healing or do you want hiding? 'Cause one requires vulnerability—and the other requires silence."

That hit Miera like a wave.

Her mother leaned in. "You've healed from heartbreak before, but have you ever let love partner with your healing?"

Miera blinked. "What do you mean?"

"I mean maybe this isn't just about trusting him again. Maybe it's about trusting you again. Trusting that God can still write beauty even when a chapter starts messy. Trusting that you're not the broken girl anymore—you're the woman who gets to choose what love looks like now."

She reached across the table, gently taking Miera's hand. "But don't you go rebuildin' anything unless God's the one handing you the bricks."

Miera closed her eyes, letting her mother's words sink in like balm to her soul.

And then... her phone rang.

The name flashed across the screen: **Fitzgerald.**

She stared at it—hands no longer trembling from fear, but from the weight of what she was carrying. The weight of *choice*.

She looked at her mother.

"I think I'm ready to hear him. Not just for what he says—but for what God wants me to discern."

Her mother nodded. "Then answer with your spirit listening louder than your ears."

Miera stepped into the other room and took a breath before answering.

"...Hello?"

His voice came through, thick and strained. "Miera. Please don't hang up. Please."

She didn't speak. Just listened.

"I—I don't even know where to start," he continued, voice ragged like he hadn't slept either. "I messed up. I should've told you. I know that. I didn't lie to hurt you—I just... I didn't know how."

"I was never trying to hide you in anyone's shadow. This house? It's not hers. It's ours. It became ours the moment you walked in."

Miera finally responded, quiet but clear. "But the door didn't change, Fitz."

There was a pause. Then a sigh. "I know. I panicked. I thought if I left the past closed, it couldn't hurt our future. But I see now... it was hurting you the whole time."

His voice cracked. "I'm not perfect. I'm learning how to lead, how to love, how to heal. But if you'll let me, I want to learn with you. I want to walk this journey—not just toward the altar, but through the mess too."

Miera felt something in her loosen.

Not because everything was fixed.

But because the foundation of something real was being laid.

Not with perfection.

But with honesty.

And that... was worth building on.

Chapter 12: Wisdom in the Waiting

"If any of you lacks wisdom, let him ask of God, who gives to all liberally and without reproach, and it will be given to him."
-James 1:5

After the call ended, Miera just sat there—phone in hand, eyes unfocused, heart thumping against her ribcage.

Fitzgerald's words echoed in her mind.

"I want to walk through everything with you—including my mess."
"I'm not perfect. I'm learning how to lead, how to love, and how to heal all at the same time."

She had heard his sincerity.

But sincerity didn't cancel pain.

And forgiveness didn't automatically rebuild trust.

She needed wisdom. *Godly* wisdom.

She grabbed her keys and made her way to the one place that had never failed her in times like this—**Mother Evelyn's house.**

Mother Evelyn was her godmother's aunt, but over the years, she had become more than that. She was a spiritual powerhouse, the kind of woman who knew how to pierce through your flesh and speak directly to your spirit. With nothing but a look and a prayer, she could snatch your soul back from confusion.

Miera pulled up to the small white house on the corner and sat for a moment before getting out. The scent of freshly baked sweet bread and peppermint tea met her at the door—along with Mother Evelyn's voice.

"I knew you were coming," she said before Miera could even knock. "The Lord showed me in prayer this morning."

Miera stepped inside and immediately felt a shift. It was as if the walls had been praying all week. Peace hung in the air like protection.

Mother Evelyn motioned to the living room. "Sit down, baby. Let's talk."

Miera sat on the edge of the couch, fingers laced, voice trembling. "I don't even know where to start."

"Start with what broke you," Mother Evelyn said, pouring two cups of tea. "Then we'll talk about what's trying to heal you."

Miera exhaled slowly. "Fitzgerald lied to me. Or maybe not outright—but he didn't tell me about his past. He let me live in a house that used to be shared with his ex-fiancée. She showed up yesterday... and the whole foundation cracked beneath me."

Mother Evelyn nodded slowly but didn't interrupt.

"I felt... humiliated. Like I was walking around in someone else's leftover promises. And the worst part?" Miera blinked back fresh tears. "I think I still want to believe him."

"Because your spirit sees what your soul hasn't caught up to yet," Mother Evelyn said gently. "But you can't build a future when the past is still hidden in the walls. What you experienced wasn't just betrayal—it was *triggers*."

Miera looked up, startled by how accurate that word was.

"You've been hurt before, haven't you?" she asked.

Miera nodded. "Yes. Deeply. And I never really healed. I just got stronger."

"Honey, strength without healing is like concrete poured over broken glass. Eventually, the cracks rise to the surface. What you're facing right now? It's not just about Fitzgerald. It's about *you* finally confronting the places you haven't let God restore."

Miera's eyes welled up again.

"But how do I know if I should try again? Or walk away?"

Mother Evelyn leaned forward, locking eyes with her. "By checking your fruit. Not your feelings."

She opened her Bible and read:

**"But the wisdom that comes from heaven is first of all pure; then
peace-loving, considerate, submissive, full of mercy and good fruit,
impartial and sincere."**
— James 3:17

"Are the actions bringing peace or confusion? Mercy or manipulation? Does the
relationship push you closer to God or pull you away?"

Miera sat back, quiet.

Then Mother Evelyn took her hand and said something Miera would never
forget:

> "Forgiveness is for *you*. Reconciliation is for *God to decide*. Your job
> isn't to glue broken pieces together—it's to ask God if the vessel is
> still part of His design."

That night, Miera journaled.

She didn't text Fitzgerald. Didn't call him back.
 Instead, she sat in her room and wrote out every prayer, every fear, every
wound... and every hope.

She closed the journal with one final line:

**"God, I'm not going to move unless You lead. But if You say walk, I'll
walk—even if it means walking away."**

Chapter 13: When a Man Kneels

"My sacrifice, O God, is a broken spirit; a broken and contrite heart you, God, will not despise."
-Psalm 51:17

Fitzgerald sat alone in his car, parked near the lakefront. The skyline blinked behind him like a slow heartbeat, but his own chest felt tight—like it hadn't exhaled since Miera walked out that door.

He had messed up.

He knew it.

But what scared him most... was that she might not come back.

He looked down at his hands—hands that could build anything, solve problems, shake deals into motion... but couldn't undo the silence between them.

God, I don't know what to say to her anymore.

He rested his head against the steering wheel, frustration mounting. "I tried to protect her. I really did."

But a whisper in his spirit pushed back:
Was it protection... or pride?

He sat up slowly.

The truth hit hard.

He didn't want to admit it—not even to God—but deep down... he was afraid. Afraid that if Miera saw *all* of his truth, she might walk away before ever fully stepping in.

And so he kept parts hidden. Not to deceive—but to delay. To manage the image.

But love isn't about image.

He knew that now.

He pulled out his phone, not to call her, but to open the Bible app. He didn't know where to start, so he just typed "repentance" into the search bar.

The first verse that came up:

> "The sacrifices of God are a broken spirit; a broken and contrite
> heart, O God, you will not despise."
> — Psalm 51:17

Fitzgerald exhaled—deep and shaky.

He hadn't been broken in a while. Not like this. And for a man who was used to being in control, this—the uncertainty, the guilt, the spiritual gut-check—was almost unbearable.

He stepped out of the car and walked toward the lake. The city behind him, the water in front.

Then he did something he hadn't done in a long time.

He dropped to his knees.

Right there in the grass, hands lifted, heart exposed.

"**God…**" he whispered, voice breaking, "I've been trying to be a man… but I realize I haven't been trying to be *Your* man. I led with what I knew—money, confidence, charm—but I failed to lead with honesty. I failed to lead with the truth. I failed to lead with *You*."

His shoulders shook as tears streamed down his face—raw, unrehearsed, unfiltered.

"I hurt her, Lord. I bruised her trust. I mishandled what I asked You for. She was an answered prayer, and I treated her like a secret I wasn't ready to live out loud."

He fell forward, hands digging into the dirt.

"Fix me, God! Not just for her—but for You. I don't want to be a man who prays well and hides worse. I don't want to lead with ego and call it strength. I want to be free—fully free. In You. Through You. For You."

He paused, sobbing openly.

Then came the words that came from a deeper place than he'd ever prayed before:

"Make me the kind of man I'd want my son to become. The kind of man I'd want my daughter to marry. Not just bold, but broken before You. Not just present—but spiritually prepared."

He stayed there for a long time—just listening. Just breathing. Just being still.

And then, like the softest wave brushing against the shore, he heard the Lord whisper:

> **"I will rebuild you with truth. But this time, from the inside out. You were never called to protect her image. You were called to protect her heart. And if I entrust her to you again, it won't be because you looked the part. It will be because you *became* it."**

Back in his car, Fitzgerald opened his notes app and began writing.

Not to defend himself.

Not to explain.

But to be *honest.*

A real man. A humbled man. A man finally stripped of image.

He ended the note with one final line:

"Whatever you decide, Miera... I thank God for the woman you are. And for the mirror you held up."

He hit send.

And this time, he didn't check to see if it was read.

He simply whispered, **"Your will be done."**
And drove home in silence.

Chapter 14: The Mirror and the Mercy

"Trust in the Lord with all your heart and lean not on your own understanding."
-Proverbs 3:5

The sun was barely up when Miera's eyes flickered open. She hadn't meant to fall asleep. Her journal was still open on her lap. The last line stared back at her like a vow:

"God, I'm not going to move unless You lead. But if You say walk, I'll walk—even if it means walking away."

Her phone buzzed softly on the nightstand. She reached for it, bracing herself.

Fitzgerald.

No text preview—just his name.

She hesitated, heart thudding like it wasn't sure if it was ready to feel again. Then she tapped it open.

It wasn't a novel. But it wasn't shallow either. It was something different.

It was the voice of a man who had knelt in the dark and come back with light.

Miera,
   I needed time to talk to God before I talked to you again.

Not to offer a defense.
But to come to you *delivered*.

I now realize I wasn't just afraid of your reaction—I was afraid of being *fully seen*. And that fear made me manage the truth instead of walking in it.

But love that hides isn't love at all. It's image management. And you... you deserve *intimacy*, not illusion.

I've spent the last 24 hours laid out before God—literally. I wept. I repented. I asked Him to remake me from the inside out.

And whether you take me back or not, I want you to know this: You were never just my answered prayer. You were also my mirror.

And that reflection showed me I still had growing to do.

So here I am... not perfect. Not polished.
But present.
If you're willing, I'd love to see you tomorrow at 6:30.
No pressure. No performance.
Just Patrice's. Just us. Just truth.

I won't move without your *yes*.

—Fitz

The tears came before she could stop them.

Because this? This didn't feel like an apology.

It felt like a *return.*

Not just of a man. But of a deeper presence. A reverence. A turning.

She clutched the phone to her chest and whispered, "God... is this You? Or am I just tired of being disappointed?"

She didn't respond right away.

Instead, she grabbed her keys and drove. No destination in mind, just a pull in her spirit.

Fifteen minutes later, she found herself in the back pew of the church where she'd first been baptized. The sanctuary was empty except for the gentle hum of the heater and the soft rays of morning light spilling through the stained-glass windows.

She walked to the altar slowly, knelt, and laid it all down.

"God," she whispered, "I'm in love with a man who wounded me... but I'm also watching You work on him. And I don't know whether to run... or rejoice."

Her voice cracked.

"Not fear of him... fear of *me.* Fear that I won't know how to believe again. How to trust again. How to build when the foundation's already been cracked."

She reached for her Bible and opened to Isaiah 43, as if led by divine hands.

Her eyes landed on:

"Forget the former things; do not dwell on the past. See, I am doing a
new thing!"
"Now it springs up; do you not perceive it? I am making a way in the
wilderness and streams in the wasteland."

A breath caught in her chest.

"Okay, God," she wept. "If You're doing a new thing… don't let me be so busy
surviving old pain that I miss new mercy. Just give me eyes to see. And courage
to follow."

Back at her car, she opened Fitzgerald's message again. This time, her fingers
didn't tremble. She knew what to say.

She replied:

Thank you.
For the honesty. For the humility. For letting me see the man behind
the mistakes.
I don't know what tomorrow looks like…
But I'm willing to sit across from you and *see it together.*
One brick at a time. One truth at a time.

Patrice's. 6:30. I'll be there.

She hit send.

Not with certainty.
But with peace.

Chapter 15: Rebuilding in the Ruins

"I also told them about the gracious hand of my God upon me and what the king had said to me. They replied, 'Let us start rebuilding.' So they began this good work."
-Nehemiah 2:18

The drive to Patrice's felt longer than usual. Miera sat in the passenger seat, silent, her hands resting on her lap. Fitzgerald glanced at her a few times, but he didn't rush the silence.

He didn't touch the radio.
He didn't fill the space with charm.
He just drove.

And that alone told her—he was different.

When they pulled up to the valet, Fitzgerald came around and opened her door like he always had. But this time, he didn't touch her waist or reach for her hand. He simply whispered, "You look beautiful," and stepped back to give her space.

Miera nodded gently. "Thank you."

Inside Patrice's, everything felt familiar—the soft jazz, the warm lighting, the scent of buttered garlic and rosemary. This was their spot. The place they used to laugh like kids and flirt like teenagers. The place where their love once felt untouched by the world.

But tonight, it all felt… layered.

They were seated at their usual booth by the window that overlooked the water.

It was quiet. Still.

Miera looked out across the river and tried to calm the war inside her.

He showed up. He humbled himself. He didn't deflect. He asked permission. He's doing it right.

And yet, part of her still felt like that little girl with a cracked heart and a million questions she was too afraid to ask.

Fitzgerald cleared his throat.

"I prayed before I came here," he said, breaking the silence.

"I did too," Miera replied without looking at him.

There was a pause—brief, but heavy.

He spoke again. "Can I ask what you prayed for?"

She looked at him then. Not through him—but at him.

"I prayed that I wouldn't come here hoping to hear what I wanted... but what I needed to hear," she said. "And that God would help me listen with my healed heart, not my hurt one."

Fitzgerald nodded slowly. "I prayed for the strength to tell the full truth... even if it cost me everything."

Miera raised a brow. "There's more?"

He sighed. "Not more secrets. Just... more of me. The part I've never really shared."

Just then, their waitress approached with water and a basket of bread. But before she placed it down, she paused.

She looked at them, brows furrowing ever so slightly. Then she smiled softly. "Excuse me... I don't usually do this, but... I just feel led to say—whatever y'all are rebuilding? God is in it. He's giving you grace for the ruins. I don't know what that means to you, but... He said to tell you: 'It won't fall this time, because now it's being built on truth.'"

She blinked like she didn't know where that came from.

"I'm sorry, that just came out," she said, almost embarrassed.

Miera and Fitzgerald sat frozen, tears instantly welling in both their eyes.

"No need to apologize," Miera whispered. "Thank you."

The waitress nodded and placed the bread down, her hands trembling slightly. "Your food will be out soon."

As she walked away, Miera exhaled deeply. "God... You really don't miss."

Fitzgerald whispered, "That was Him. That was all Him."

Silence lingered again, but now it felt holy.

When the waitress disappeared, Fitzgerald leaned forward.

"I was raised to believe that a real man protects. He provides. He performs. So that's who I became. I learned how to show up. How to shine. How to win. But I never learned how to tell the truth in the middle of my brokenness."

Miera stayed still, listening.

"When Jasmin and I ended," he continued, "I buried it. Fast. Never looked back. So when I met you, I convinced myself I had healed just because I had moved on."

He shook his head.

"But healing without honesty? It's just high-functioning hurt."

Miera's eyes glossed over. That hit too close.

"I didn't tell you about the house because I didn't want to reopen something I had worked hard to forget," he said. "But I should've remembered that love built on lies can't stand in storms."

There was another pause.

Then Miera spoke.

"You know what's wild?" she said, finally looking him directly in the eyes. "All this time, I've been carrying around my own hidden chapter. Not a secret fiancé—but a betrayal that cut so deep I stopped trusting my instincts. I thought I healed from it... but when Jasmin showed up, all those feelings came back. And I didn't just see her. I saw him. The one before you."

Fitzgerald's face softened with surprise.

"I've been blaming you for opening a wound I never fully closed," she continued. "And that's not fair."

The moment between them cracked open—soft, raw, real.

The waitress returned with their food, but neither touched their plates.

"I don't want a perfect love," Miera whispered. "I want an honest one."

"I don't want to perform anymore," Fitzgerald said. "I want to be known—even in the places that scare me."

Another pause.
This time filled with peace.

Then, unexpectedly, Fitzgerald pulled a folded paper from his inside jacket pocket and laid it on the table.

Miera looked at it, confused. "What is this?"

"A lease," he said. "For a new place."

Her brows furrowed. "You're moving?"

"If we're going to rebuild," he said slowly, "I don't want it to be in a house built on someone else's history. That house has too many shadows. You deserve light. We do."

Miera's heart swelled.

"You'd do that?" she asked.

"I already did," he replied. "If you say yes, we'll start fresh—new space, new memories, new covenant. If you say no... I'll still go. Because I need to become the man I prayed to be, with or without the reward of your presence."

Silence again.
But this time, it wasn't tense.
It was full.

Miera sat back, the weight of everything hitting her.

He didn't come just to fix.
He came to rebuild.
And not just their love—but himself.

She reached across the table and gently placed her hand over his.

And just like that, peace flooded the space.

"I'm willing," she said, eyes steady. "To rebuild. To begin again. Slowly. Honestly. Together."

Fitzgerald let out a long breath he didn't even know he was holding.

"Thank You, God," he whispered.

Chapter 16: Brick by Brick (Even in the Rain)

"Therefore everyone who hears these words of mine and puts them into practice is like a wise man who built his house on the rock. The rain came down, the streams rose, and the winds blew and beat against that house; yet it did not fall, because it had its foundation on the rock."
-Matthew 7:24-25

Two months later.

The air smelled like fall—crisp, earthy, and quietly shifting. Miera stood outside the front door of a townhouse tucked on a quiet block just west of downtown. It was modest. Beautiful. Full of windows that welcomed light in.

No shadows here.

She sipped from the warm cup in her hand and looked down at the welcome mat:
"Grace lives here."

Fitzgerald had picked it out.

The door opened right on time.

He smiled, softer this time. "Come in, Mi."

Miera stepped inside and looked around again, even though she'd already visited a few times. Somehow, it still caught her off guard—the peace of it. The space was minimal but intentional. Ivory walls. Clean lines. Cozy furniture.

Scripture-lined artwork that felt like whispered prayers:

"As for me and my house..."
"Love covers."
"He restores."

"I kept it light," Fitzgerald said, rubbing the back of his neck. "In case you wanted to add your touch later."

She gave a small smile. "I like it. Feels... safe."

There was no pressure. No forced affection.
Just presence. Partnership. Peace.

They had spent the last two months going slow—*intentionally* slow.

No sleepovers. No blurred lines.
Just conversations.
Prayer.
Counseling.
Healing.

Each week, they met with Pastor Langston—a faith-based counselor who didn't let either of them hide behind potential or pretend.

He'd say things like:
- "You can't build a new future using the language of your broken past."

- "Trust doesn't grow from promises. It grows from patterns."
- "A healed heart can't be rushed. It has to be reintroduced to safety."

And slowly, **brick by brick**, they began doing the work.

That night, Miera curled up on the couch while Fitzgerald pulled out a notebook.

"Are you ready?" he asked.

She raised a brow. "You know I love structure."

They both laughed gently.

Each week, they did the same healing exercise Pastor Langston gave them:
✦ One truth about your past.
✦ One truth about your present.
✦ One hope for your future.

Fitzgerald started.

"Past truth: I didn't know how to lead without controlling.
Present truth: I'm learning that surrender isn't weakness—it's obedience.
Future hope: That I'll be a man my future wife doesn't have to recover from."

Miera's breath caught.

She nodded slowly, then opened her own notebook.

"Past truth: I carried trust issues dressed up as 'intuition.'
Present truth: I'm not afraid to say when I'm scared anymore.
Future hope: That I'll be free to love without always bracing for betrayal."

The words lingered in the space between them like incense.

"Thank you for being honest," he said.

"I spent so many years being strong," Miera said quietly. "But this? This is harder. Being soft again. Open."

"You don't have to be strong all the time with me," he replied. "Just honest."

She looked up, eyes warm but steady. "I don't want to rush us. I know everyone expects us to go back to what we were... but I don't want that."

"Me neither," he said, shaking his head. "That version of us looked good. But this version?" He reached for her hand. "This feels good. Feels... *true.*"

She squeezed his fingers. "I need you to pursue me. Not just romantically. But spiritually. Consistently. Like the man you said you're becoming."

"I will," he said. "Even on the days you don't feel lovable. Even when we disagree. I'll still choose you—and I'll choose to pray first."

She smiled. "Then I'll choose to show up—even when I'm scared."

He grinned. "As you should."

Later that evening, Fitzgerald walked her to her car. The street was quiet, leaves dancing across the sidewalk. No dramatic music. No emotional goodbyes. Just *them*—simple, growing, and safe.

As she reached for her door, Miera turned.

"You know what I've learned?" she said.

"What?"

"That love doesn't mean there won't be cracks. It just means we choose to rebuild anyway."

Fitz nodded, his voice low but steady. "And I'll lay every brick with you. One by one. Even when it's hard. Even when it's slow."

He didn't kiss her.

He didn't need to.

He just held her hand for a moment longer than usual... and let her go.

Chapter 17: This Time, Forever

"It always protects, always trusts, always hopes, always perseveres."
-1 Corinthians 13:7

Miera had no idea what was planned.

All she knew was her mom told her to be ready by 5:30, to wear something "soft and royal," and that "lip gloss and lotion were non-negotiables."

The text from her sister Lola had simply read:
"We got plans. Be fine. Period."

Miera rolled her eyes but couldn't fight the smile pulling at her lips. Something was up.

When she walked out of her house, a sleek black SUV was waiting. The driver greeted her by name and opened the door with a smile.

As they pulled off, she noticed the route looked familiar—but it wasn't until they turned onto the lakefront that her heart started to race.

She sat up straighter as the car slowed near a private pier—beautifully lit with white twinkle lights, candle-lined walkways, and soft music playing from somewhere hidden in the breeze.

And then she saw him.

Fitzgerald.

Standing at the end of the dock, dressed in all black, his smile as wide and warm as ever. The kind of smile that said: *I see you. I choose you. I honor you.*

The driver opened her door, and Miera stepped out, every part of her body tingling with anticipation. The closer she walked, the more she noticed: fresh flowers, printed photos of their journey clipped to golden string lights, and off to the side, their entire family—smiling, clapping, holding in their screams.

Her daddy was already tearing up.
Her mama was fanning herself with her clutch.
And her sisters... oh, her sisters were doing the absolute most.

"Girl, don't trip in those heels!" Kiesha shouted.

Lila added, "We need pictures, not a rescue mission!"

And of course, Lola brought the grand finale:
"Just when I was about to open my new business... y'all tried to make my business fold!" she yelled, tossing her hands dramatically.

Everyone roared with laughter—including Miera, who covered her mouth, laughing and crying all at once.

Fitzgerald chuckled and met her halfway down the dock.

"I needed the village here this time," he said softly, eyes never leaving hers. "Because you've always said love isn't just about the couple—it's about community. And I wanted our people to witness the *promise* this time."

He led her to the center, where a small stage had been set. With trembling hands, he reached into his coat pocket and pulled out a small velvet box.

"But before I ask you anything," he said, turning to their families, "there's something I need to say."

He looked at her parents first.

"Mr. and Mrs. Nielsen... Thank you for your grace. Thank you for not shutting the door before God had the final word. I know I had to earn my place again—and I'm still earning it—but thank you for letting God do the rebuilding."

Her father stepped forward, eyes glassy. "Son, real men fall. But the ones worth keeping... they get back up—with *God* in front and *humility* in hand. I see you now. And I trust the God in you."

Her mother smiled through tears. "We've been praying for this love to mature. We're standing behind it now—stronger than ever."

Then, Fitzgerald turned back to Miera.

"Mi... we've been through enough to write a book and start a ministry," he said with a gentle laugh. "But what I've learned is that love isn't about perfection—it's about pursuit. Of truth. Of healing. Of *you.*"

He got down on one knee, the box now open, revealing a radiant-cut diamond nestled in a gold band—elegant, strong, full of light.

"Miera Nielsen... my best friend, my answered prayer, my second chance... will you marry me? *This time, for forever.*"

Miera blinked back a flood of tears.

And for just one second—everything else faded.

The crowd. The lights. The pressure.

She thought about the tears she'd sown on her pillow.
The healing she fought for.
The prayers she once thought God had ignored.

And then...

An older woman—someone she didn't recognize—stood near the back of the crowd and spoke softly, yet clearly:

"The Lord says this is not just restoration—this is divine release. This is what happens when two people don't just reconcile, but resurrect."

The moment stilled.

Even the wind quieted.

And Miera knew... this was holy ground.

"Yes!" she cried, laughing through her tears. "A thousand times, yes!"

The family erupted in cheers.
Lila hit a high note she had no business attempting.
Kiesha started a praise dance in heels.
And Lola? Still recording. Still extra. Still hilarious:
"Y'all had me stressed! IDK if this was the *final season,* or we doing *spinoffs*?"

Fitzgerald stood, slipped the ring on her finger, and wrapped her in the kind of hug that felt like home and heaven in one embrace.

Later that evening, the celebration continued on a private rooftop nearby. Candlelight danced in the breeze. Plates clinked. Laughter spilled like wine. There was no tension. No shade. Just **grace in action**.

Even Miera's younger cousins hugged Fitzgerald and whispered things like:

"You better not mess this up again, Unc," and
"We like you now—so don't get dropped."

Fitzgerald laughed, owned it, and received every piece of love—and every roast.

As the evening settled and the stars crept out over the skyline, Miera stood at the railing, looking out over the city that raised her.

Fitzgerald came behind her and wrapped his arms around her waist.

"I'm not just building a life with you," he whispered. "I'm building a legacy—with you at the center and God at the head."

Miera leaned back into him and smiled.

"We've already started," she said.
"Brick by brick. This time, forever."

Chapter 18: The Day Love Stood Still

"See, I am doing a new thing! Now it springs up; do you not perceive it? I am making a way in the wilderness and streams in the wasteland."
Isaiah 43:19

The sun rose slowly and golden over the quiet countryside estate where Miera and Fitzgerald would become one.

The air was warm with grace.
The breeze? Soft, almost sacred.
And inside the bridal suite?

Controlled chaos wrapped in beauty.

Miera stood in front of the floor-length mirror in a satin robe embroidered with *Mrs. Godfrey-To-Be*, surrounded by her sisters and the women who had prayed, danced, cried, and clowned with her through every season.

Lola, of course, was doing the absolute most.

"Okay, who's gonna tell Miera her eyelash is already trying to wave goodbye?" she said, tissue in one hand, humor in the other.

"I'm not crying," Miera sniffled.

"Girl," Lila grinned, tilting her head. "You say that, but your face is testifying otherwise."

Everyone cracked up.

Kiesha came in with a tray of mini cinnamon rolls. "Eat before you faint in front of the Pastor. You know he doesn't pause mid-vow for snacks."

Nola grabbed Miera's hand. "You ready?"

Miera looked around. Her mother was in the corner fixing her veil with quiet care. Her nieces twirled in their flower girl dresses, giggling as they made a mess of their petals—for the third time. Her sisters were both excited and calm in the best way.

And her?

She felt peace.

"I'm not just ready," she whispered. "I'm sure."

The Ceremony

The sanctuary was a dream come to life. White drapes spilled from the ceiling like ribbons of light. Candles lined the aisle in delicate glass towers. Roses—soft blush, ivory, and gold—wrapped the altar like the garden of Eden had bloomed overnight.

When the doors opened and Miera stepped forward on her father's arm, time slowed.

She looked like redemption.
Like every answered prayer that had ever waited its turn.
Fitzgerald's eyes filled instantly. His breath hitched. His knees buckled slightly.
Pastor Langston leaned in and whispered with a grin, "Not yet, son."

As Miera reached the altar, her father kissed her forehead, placed her hand in Fitzgerald's, and said with authority, "Take care of my girl."

"I will forever," Fitzgerald said. But it wasn't just the words. It was the way he looked at her.

Still holding her hand, he leaned in and whispered low enough for only her to hear:

"I'll carry your joy like treasure.
And your pain like armor.
I'll hold your laughter like a promise,
and your tears like a vow."

A tear slid down Miera's cheek, but she didn't look away.

Then, the atmosphere shifted.

Pastor Langston didn't preach—he released.

"This is not a love story. This is an assignment.
God trusted two imperfect people with kingdom territory—and today, He's establishing a covenant.
Not for comfort, but for calling."

They exchanged handwritten vows—**raw, holy, and laced with tears**.

And when the pastor finally said, *"You may now kiss your bride,"* Fitzgerald didn't just kiss her.

He covered her.

And the whole room stood to its feet—clapping, praising, shouting, weeping. You could feel angels rejoicing.

Because this wasn't just a wedding.

It was a revival.

The Reception

The ballroom glowed golden with joy. Every table was candlelit. Every chair draped in elegance. Laughter spilled from every corner like confetti.

The food? Unmatched.
The dessert table? A problem.
The cake? Seven tiers of "Won't He do it."

Lola took the mic first, naturally.

"I'm Lola," she said with flair, "the one who's been emotionally invested in this relationship like I got stock in it. And trust me, I almost pulled out!"

Everyone howled.

"But today? Today I'm standing ten toes behind this marriage. Fitz, I was ready to fight you. Now I'm ready to pray for you. That's growth, okay?"

More laughter. Miera covered her face, laughing and crying all over again.

Kiesha stepped up with soft power. "Miera, I've watched you bloom even in hard soil. And Fitz—you watered that bloom with growth, not just gifts. Keep showing up."

Then came Nola. No mic. Just tears and a full heart.

"We have dreamed of this day since we were kids. But sis... you didn't just dream. You waited. You healed. You grew. And you made space for God to outdo your expectations."

Miera stood up and hugged her.

Even the uncles were in rare form—dancing in shiny loafers, starting line dances with no rhythm, raising their glasses like they were auditioning for wedding commercials.

The kids chased bubbles in their dress shoes. Aunties made everyone take 75 pictures. Cousins grilled Fitzgerald with playful warnings: "We got saved and baptized, but we still got hands, bruh."

He laughed. He thanked them. He received every joke with humility.

The Send-Off

Later, under the stars, Fitzgerald took Miera's hand and led her outside to the open field lit with lanterns and soft jazz playing through hidden speakers.

Fireworks burst above them as guests surrounded them with cheers.

"I'll never stop pursuing you," he whispered, forehead to hers.

"And I'll never stop choosing you," she replied, her voice full and steady.

They got into the car, petals raining, laughter echoing.

And from somewhere in the crowd, you already know it came—

"OKAY, now I'm officially off-duty!" Lola yelled. "Y'all BETTER be together forever because my edges can't handle another breakup!"

The crowd roared.

And as the car pulled away, hands entwined and hearts finally whole, Miera laid her head on Fitzgerald's shoulder and whispered:

"This isn't just a wedding. It's a resurrection."

And just like that...

Love stood still.

But only for a moment—
 Before it ran full speed into forever.

Chapter 19: The Becoming of Us

"Being confident of this, that he who began a good work in you will carry it on to completion until the day of Christ Jesus."
Philippians 1:6

Nobody tells you how loud silence feels after the wedding.

No more congratulations.
No more group chats exploding with dress links and color swatches.
Just two toothbrushes.
One closet.
And a whole lot of learning how to live in love, not just fall in it.

Miera stood barefoot in the kitchen, wearing Fitzgerald's hoodie, staring at a coffee pot that clearly wasn't brewing.
"You didn't refill the filter," she called out.

From the bathroom, he yelled, "You didn't take the chicken out like I asked!"

They met eyes in the hallway—his toothbrush still foaming, her arms crossed, eyebrow raised.
And just like that...

They were in it.

Marriage.

Not the honeymoon reel.
Not the Instagram highlight.
The real thing.

Their first month was sweet chaos and silent agreements.
Fitz would randomly pull her into his arms and whisper, "I still can't believe I get to love you like this."

Miera would smile and think, Neither can I. Not after all I've survived.

They prayed together.
Sometimes they fell asleep mid-prayer.
Sometimes they fell apart mid-sentence—and into each other's arms.
It was beautiful.
Messy.
Holy.

But by month three?

Life hit.

Bills didn't care about their wedding photos.
Schedules clashed like cymbals.
Groceries went missing.
Arguments came hard and fast—then left silence in their wake.

One night, a fight about towels somehow spiraled into a three-day emotional shutdown.

Miera sat on the edge of their bed, tears tracing her cheekbones, wondering, Did we miss God?

Fitz walked in, saw her posture—shoulders slumped like her spirit—and dropped his pride.
No script. No apology template. Just truth.

"I know we said forever," he said, "but nobody told me forever would mean dying to myself daily."

She nodded, eyes red. "And nobody told me that loving you would reveal all the places in me still unhealed."

They didn't speak after that.
They just held each other.
No music. No filters. Just raw, warm becoming.

By month six, something started to shift.

They found rhythm.
They laughed again.
They repented quicker.

They held weekly devotionals—sometimes at home, sometimes walking by the lake.

They accidentally started a couples' group at church that became a monthly ministry.
They replaced pride with prayer.
Perfection with presence.

Miera stopped assuming every disagreement meant abandonment.
Fitzgerald stopped thinking leadership required control.

They fought with grace.
Loved with fire.
And slowly built something that wasn't just sacred...

It was sustainable.

One night, after a deep conversation about legacy and legacy launch pads, Miera curled into Fitzgerald's chest.

He whispered, "I feel like God's about to birth something through us."

Miera smiled. "Me too. I feel it in my womb—not just naturally, but spiritually. It's like something's kicking."

He grinned. "So you saying we should... practice for the natural part?"

"Boy, if you don't—!"

They burst into the kind of laughter only covenant makes room for.
Laughter laced with safety. Joy rooted in soil they both once thought was too
cracked to grow anything.

A quiet night.
Rain tapping gently against the window panes.
The glow of a single lamp.

Miera curled in Fitzgerald's arms, both of them wrapped in a worn fleece
blanket, faces peaceful.

No TV.
No background noise.
Just heartbeats and home.

She whispered, "Whatever God births through us next... whether it's a child, a
business, or a calling... I know now we're strong enough to carry it."

Fitzgerald kissed her temple.
"We're not just building a marriage," he whispered back.
"We're building a movement."

And as the moment settles, the screen fades to black...

A ding breaks the silence.
A **positive pregnancy test** peeks out from Miera's purse on the table.
Next to it?

A flyer for the launch of their new ministry: The Altar Between Us.
And a notification flashes across her phone:

New Email from: Elevate Publishing Group
 Subject: We'd love to discuss turning your love story into a book series...

TO BE CONTINUED.

A Letter to You, Beloved Reader

Dear Beautiful Soul,

If you're reading this, let me first say this: **you are seen, known, and fiercely loved**—by God and by the version of yourself that's still becoming.

This story? It wasn't just fiction.
It was an invitation.
An invitation to believe in the **realness of redemption**, in the beauty of becoming, and in the kind of love that heaven still writes.

I don't know your current season.
Maybe you're single and wondering if love is still possible.
Maybe you're married and fighting silent battles that no one sees.
Maybe you've been divorced and feel like your chance has expired.
Or maybe your heart is scared—because trusting again feels like handing someone a map to all your most tender places.

But let me prophesy this over you right now:

God is not finished writing your story.

Love is not lost to you.

You are not too broken to be built with.
You are not too late to be loved well.
You are not too far from the kind of healing that can hold love without fear.

If God could raise Lazarus after four days, He can resurrect the buried hope in your heart.

If He can redeem Peter after denial, He can restore you after disappointment.

You serve a God who specializes in shattered things.

Marriage isn't just about romance—it's about **assignment**.

It's not about perfection—it's about **partnership**.

And unity? It isn't always easy.

But it is always **worth fighting for** when God's hands are the ones holding it together.

To the one who's afraid to love again:

God is not asking you to be fearless—only faithful.

To the one who's in a rough season of marriage:

It's okay to pause and pray. It's okay to rebuild. And yes, it's okay to seek help.

Don't suffer in silence. Let love be **louder than ego**.

To the one who feels forgotten:

God knows your name. He knows your tears. And He's not just preparing a partner—He's preparing **you** for **purposeful love**.

So here's my word for you:

This is not the end. This is preparation.

God is raising up healed hearts, holy unions, and revival-filled marriages.

And your name is still on Heaven's guest list.

Don't rush the next chapter.
Don't fear the waiting room.
Just make space in your spirit for the kind of love that doesn't just make you feel
safe...
but makes you feel seen.

I speak this over you now:

💍 Restoration.
🔥 Clarity.
🕊 Peace.
💧 Healing.
🌱 And fresh oil for every dry place.

May God prepare your heart for **legacy**, not just love.
May you fall in love with wholeness before you fall in love with another person.
And may your yes to love—when it comes—be filled with boldness,
discernment, and divine timing.

With love, fire, and full expectation,
Muriel Nelson-Godfrey
Speaker of Life. Prophetess. Sister in the trenches. Witness of real love.

www.ingramcontent.com/pod-product-compliance
Lightning Source LLC
Chambersburg PA
CBHW071438260626
47170CB00008B/2765